Great Minds Think Alike

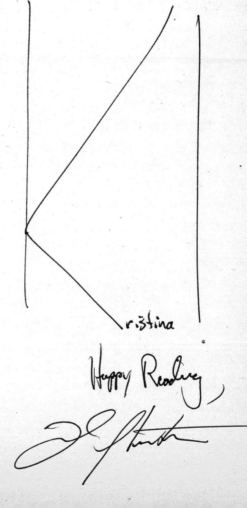

To

Kristina

Happy Reading

Great Minds Think Alike

Ted Staunton

Canadian Cataloguing in Publication Data

Staunton, Ted, 1956-
  Great minds think alike

ISBN 0-9699926-1-0

I. Title.

PS8587.T334G74 1989 jC813'.54 C89-094339-7
PZ7.S73Gr 1989

Printed and bound in Canada by Webcom Ltd.
Cover design by N.R. Jackson
Edited by Charis Wahl
Typeset by Pixel Graphics Inc.

89 0 9 8 7 6 5 4 3 2

For Will, who got here just in time
and to Charis Wahl with many thanks.

Contents

Gift Trapped

"**W**HAT DO TWO-TON CANARIES SAY?"
"I don't know. What?"
"Here kitty, kitty."

"Ohhphbb." I snorted and snickered at the same time. It was after dinner. Maggie and I were sitting on my front porch, spying on Russell Hummaker, Maggie's worst enemy, and reading a riddle book.

All down Greenapple Street you could see people on their porches or watering their gardens. The sky was turning orange behind the trees. Lawn mowers were humming. It was summer almost – only six school days left, which should have been excellent. But this summer meant problems as big as a two-ton canary: Mr. Flynn going, Great Aunt Gertrude coming, and Russell staying forever.

Thinking about it made me feel like I just swallowed a bag of lemons.

The news about Mr. Flynn was bugging me most. We'd had him for our teacher for two years and now he was leaving, to teach at another school next fall. Just like that. We'd never see him again.

I was never a big star in his class, not like Maggie

and Russell, but I did *some* special things ... I guess, maybe. I wanted to anyway, because Mr. Flynn did amazing stuff. He was always joking and twirling his big moustache till it nearly poked him in the eye, or telling us about going scuba diving or camping or travelling to neat places. He even let us do okay junk in class sometimes.

I wanted to make a great surprise that he'd know was mine even when I never said so. My best idea was to get him some amazing present, like for diving or exploring, but I didn't know what to get. Even if I wanted help – and I didn't – there was nothing I could do. My mom was busy at her school, my dad never did Mr. Flynn-type stuff, and Maggie was always spying on Russell. I was stuck and time was running out.

I was going to school early and asking to help and putting my hand up and hanging around till late, but who cared about that stuff? I needed something great. Instead I was down to hoping I'd find an extra-good riddle to tell him.

Maggie handed me the riddle book and sank down in her chair until the top of her head barely cleared the arms. Her legs stretched out above her until her red running shoes sat on the porch railing. With her feet poking up, she looked like a human periscope. I smooshed my chair closer until I could reach the railing too. Maggie wasn't going to be the Maple Avenue Marvel *and* taller than me. Or not much taller, anyway.

I flipped through the book.

"How do you stop a charging rhino? Take away its credit card!"

I laughed. Maggie didn't.

I flipped more pages.

"Why should you always take a baseball player camping with you?"

No answer.

I looked up. Maggie wasn't even listening. She was peering between the bars of the railing. Bobby and Tracey and Leanne had left their bikes in Russell's driveway and were following him into the back yard.

"Traitors," Maggie snapped. The lemons plopped back into my stomach and I made a squinched-up face. Tree house trouble again. See, Russell lived in Maggie's old house from before she moved to Maple Avenue and he was always saying how he was going to tear down Maggie's tree house in the back yard. The tree house was Maggie's favourite place in the whole world and Russell cut it up like baloney just to bug her. It was bad enough that we'd shovelled snow all winter to get money to build a new one, and then spent it somehow. It was just as bad that we had to spy till Maggie made a new plan against Russell. But now Maggie was spying instead of what she was supposed to be doing – saving me from Great Aunt Gertrude.

My mom's Aunt Gertrude, the scariest person in my whole family, was coming to visit for two weeks at the end of July. Just the thought of it made my toes scrunch up. She'd probably glare at me across the dining-room table for not eating my lima beans, like she did when I was a little kid. You could tell she liked lima beans better than kids. I tried not to imagine the rest of her visit, except for her ear lobes. They were the longest in the world, even my mom said so.

Maggie had promised to help me escape Great Aunt Gertrude, but that was before Russell started inviting everyone but us over to play in the tree house. Maggie said that meant war.

Well, I thought, at least this time she wasn't dragging me into DaCostas' back yard so she could spy with binoculars. That was scary. I'd never known their dog was that big.

"Hey, are you going to listen or what?" I complained.

"In a sec. I'm just getting those names." Maggie wrote down who went into Russell's back yard in this little note pad she'd carried ever since she read some book about a girl spy. Then she looked at her watch and wrote down the time, too. "Okay," she said, "what's the riddle again?"

"Why should you always take a baseball player camping with you? Give up? So you'll have someone to pitch the tent!"

"What a groaner." Before I could ask another one Maggie said, "That's what we need, huh? A tent. We could move it around wherever we want and they'd be stuck in the same old tree house. Or we could – "

"Or we could *give it to Mr. Flynn*," I whispered to myself. It was the most incredibly fantastic genius-type idea I'd ever had.

The lemons in my stomach turned into lemonade, just like that. It was the perfect gift. Mr. Flynn had told us he was going camping this summer and that his tent leaked. In a flash I saw it all: the last day of school, Mr. Flynn opening the tent all wrapped up in fancy paper, asking whose idea it was, everybody pushing me up to the front, and me saying, "Aw, it was nothing," and then Mr. Flynn twirling up his moustache and inviting me to come camping. I almost laughed out loud.

"I wonder how much they cost?" I asked. Maggie was still blabbing away, not even noticing me.

She sighed. "More than we've got."

"Yeah," I said, planning. "But everybody in class would pay some."

Maggie looked at me like my brains had leaked out. "Why would everyone in class pay for my tent?"

"Not yours," I shouted. "Mr. Flynn's!" And I told her my plan except for the part about how I'd be the hero.

"Not bad, Cyril," Maggie said. "I would have thought of that if I wasn't so busy with Russell. But I'd still rather get a tent for us."

"Okay, okay," I pleaded. "But Mr. Flynn's first. Please? Partners? Come on, I'm helping you with Russell." Maggie didn't answer. "Maybe," I was thinking really fast, "maybe Mr. Flynn would loan it to us, if he knew it was from us, when we – when *he* gets back from camping."

"Well … " Maggie bit her lip. "Okay. But if something happens with Russell, that comes first. And you'll have to do what I say."

"Yeah, yeah, sure," I said, not caring now that we were in business.

Well, almost. The next minute Maggie said, "Oh-oh, Cyril, this might be trouble. Your dad's going over there."

My dad had been coming along Greenapple Street with a bag from the milk store, but Russell's mom had called to him from her front door and he was walking over. They looked pretty weird. My dad had on the jeans and sweatshirt he always wore unless he had to go interview somebody for the newspaper, but Russell's mom was all fancied up. She once told my mom that when you're in real estate you have to dress for success.

She gave my dad a little card and blabbered away a mile a minute. My dad started backing down the driveway, nodding his head. She hurried right after him, still yakking.

"This looks suspicious," Maggie hissed. She reached for her notebook, never taking her eyes off them. Russell's mom was world famous for giving out her little cards to everybody that came within ten miles of her, in case they wanted to buy a house or something. My parents said if we saw her enough we could wallpaper a room with them.

I said, "Come on, she's probably just trying to sell him a swamp." My dad always said Russell's mom tried to sell swamp land in Florida and refrigerators at the North Pole.

"Well, find out," Maggie said, scribbling in her notebook. "Here he comes. Quick!" She slapped the book shut and sat on it.

But I had something way more important to ask. As he came up the steps I said, "Hey dad, how much do tents cost?"

"Tents!" My dad pretended to shudder. "I wouldn't know a tent from this plastic bag, Cyril, except I'd rather have the bag. Better ask your mom, she used to be a real camper. Used pine trees for toothpicks and all that." Then he was gone into the house.

"Cyril!" Maggie glared at me.

"Next time," I said, hardly listening. "Come on, let's ask my mom about the tent."

"Promise you'll ask your dad about Russell's mom? Cross your heart and hope to die?"

"I promise, I promise." I reached for the door.

When we explained what we wanted, my mom spread some catalogues out on the dining-room table. The tents were amazing, all bubbles and points and colours. Maggie was practically drooling, imagining them in her yard. I was practically drooling, imagining Mr. Flynn and me showing one to the class. The problem was they all cost about a jillion dollars. My mom turned a page. "Ah hah, here we go." There was a picture of a little blue tent with a red flap stretched over the top.

"Let's see." My mom read quickly. "Plastic bottom, a fly sheet – that's the red thing, keeps you dry if it rains – back vent, sleeps two."

"Perfect," I breathed.

"Mm-hmm," my mom nodded. "Might be a little small, but he and Mrs. Flynn should be okay in it."

"Mrs. Flynn?"

"She might want to go camping, too," my mom smiled.

"Oh." I hadn't thought about Mrs. Flynn. I'd have to think of something else for her to do if I went camping.

"And best of all," my mom pointed, "it's the right price."

OUTDOOR ECONOMY, it read, WITH FLY, $32.99. There were twenty-nine of us in Room 7. My mom said everybody would have to give about a dollar and a quarter to have enough, with tax and all. She helped us write a note asking everybody in class to bring money by Friday if they wanted to help. My dad typed it up. The school secretary could copy it on a machine in the morning.

When we were done, I felt so good I didn't even complain when Maggie led me back out to spy on Russell. "And don't forget to ask your dad about Mrs. Hummaker," Maggie reminded, just like I was a little kid.

I moaned. What I really wanted was to ask my mom about when she used to go camping.

For the next few days though I was too busy thinking. I got copies of the note and Maggie helped me pass them around and collect the money, all in secret from Mr. Flynn. By Friday we had everybody's but Russell's. He said he wasn't going to give us any because Mr. Flynn was crummy compared to his old teacher. "Oh yeah," Lester said, "then how come you're such a browner, huh? 'Mr. Flynn! Oooh, ooh, Mr. Flynn!' " Lester waved his hand and jumped around like Russell wanting to answer a question. Then Monica said, "And how come your mom came in to talk to Mr. Flynn about how great he was?" I almost said, "Because she wanted to sell him swamp land." I remembered her cooing away and giving him a card, but then I had a better idea: "Because she wants to get an A for the browner." It probably was the real reason too. Russell just lifted his nose higher in the air. "I already get A's."

Then Maggie said, "Why don't we just tell Mr. Flynn Russell didn't want to help?" That did it. Sucky Russell caved in like a boulder fell on him – except he never did give us the money. He kept saying he forgot, but he was just being a jerkface.

In the end it didn't really matter because my dad gave us five dollars to make sure. He said he didn't like for anyone to sleep in a tent but he didn't want Mr. Flynn to have to go without one either.

On Saturday my mom took me to get the tent and a card. I spent most of the weekend imagining Mr. Flynn and me camping in the mountains with the new tent, battling avalanches and hiking right to Alaska. Mrs. Flynn couldn't come because she didn't feel like it – and besides she was doing secret science stuff for the government. By Sunday night, Mr. Flynn and I were at the North Pole. There were two-and-a-half school days left.

Monday and Tuesday we did clean-ups in Room 7, had a baseball game, nearly finished a book Mr. Flynn was reading to us, and even did some work. Mr. Flynn had to ask us to keep the noise down about eight hundred times, but how could anyone keep quiet so close to summer? Bikes. Popsicles. Tree climbing, running through sprinklers, swimming. Plus I was doing something special for Mr. Flynn and everybody was going to see. I felt like a tin of pop all fizzed up before you open it.

On Tuesday night Maggie came over to help wrap the tent in a box and fancy paper. It was already folded up in a blue carrying sack.

The first thing Maggie said was, "Have you asked your dad yet?"

I'd forgotten. Maggie got all huffy and puffy and started complaining. "I'll *ask*," I moaned. "I promised, didn't I?"

My mom had the wrapping stuff out in the dining room. She had a gift too, for someone leaving her school. It was in a purple plastic bag and when Maggie asked what it was, she said, "Have a look."

I opened the bag but all I could see were little bits of shiny leopard-skin cloth. Maggie took them out and dangled them in her fingers.

"Ho-lee," I gulped. Maggie's face got red and we started to giggle. It was a tiny bikini bathing suit.

My mom laughed, "Hot stuff, hmmmm?" We couldn't stop giggling.

Maggie snorted, "It looks so dumb!"

"Wellll," my mom lifted her eyebrows way up, but smiling, so you knew she was just pretending to argue, "it won't be long till you two think this is quite a racy number."

"No *way*." We made pukey noises.

"Oh, we'll see. You'll like the spicy bits too. But this time it's a joke. Someone else is bringing the real gift. When you finish wrapping the tent, you can help me disguise this alluring little tidbit so it's big and heavy." She put the bikini back in its bag and dropped it into a big box.

As we worked I asked my mom, "Were you really a camper?"

She smiled. "Absolutely. All the time when I was a girl, and through university too. In fact, you know who used to take me camping when I was little? Great Aunt Gertrude."

"*Really?*"

"Yup. She and Uncle Stan. We went to cottages, too."

In my mind I saw Great Aunt Gertrude all dressed up, with her ears hanging to her waist, sitting in a canoe. Then I saw her at the dining-room table except the table was in the woods by a campfire. She was glaring at my mom, who was two feet high, and making her eat lima beans.

"Did she make you eat lima beans?"

My mom laughed. "Nope, but she showed me how to clean a fish and made me do it after that."

This time I saw Great Aunt Gertrude in her pearls and everything, but she had a butcher knife in her hand.

"But she's too old," I said.

"She hasn't always been the same age, dear, and she's not exactly ancient now. You'll see when she comes to visit. I'll bet she gives you a run for your money."

The whole thing was making me feel lemony again, so I asked about something else. "How come we don't go camping?"

"Mainly because your dad hates it." My mom looked like she was trying not to laugh. "We went camping once, before you were born. We went out to an island in a lake up north. Your dad had never even canoed before. Well, he tipped the canoe and everything got soaked and that night there was a terrible, scary electrical storm and it rained all the next day. Dad was so grumpy, we've never gone since." My mom was chuckling and Maggie smiled, but I wasn't sure. Was it okay for my mom to tell bad stuff about my dad to Maggie and me? Anyway, my mom winked and said maybe one of these days we'd drag my dad out again.

We set the two packages side by side on the dining-room table. They looked excellent. My mom's package was as big as ours, but hers was blue and ours was green. Everything was ready.

That night I didn't think I'd ever get to sleep. I lay there thinking about our gift plan. We knew we were going to have lemonade and cookies at the end of the morning, so when everybody had their lemonade Maggie was going to play this tape she had where all these trumpets blare for an announcement. Next Monica, the biggest mouth in class, would jump up and say, "Mr. Flynn, we interrupt this party for a special presentation." And then, when it was real quiet I'd take the gift up to the front, give it to Mr. Flynn with everyone watching, and say, "Mr. Flynn, this is from all of us." Everybody would cheer and he'd open it.

That was as far as we planned, but I knew the rest. When he opened the package I'd be right there for him to thank and ask me camping. It was going to be perfect.

And after that, summer. Tomorrow. I squirmed and yawned to see if I was tired. Not yet. A car went by and then I heard one pull in and stop. Its door slammed. My dad must be home. A few seconds later a lawn chair scraped on the patio and I heard my dad's voice quietly from the back yard. My mom's voice floated softly back. They talked for awhile, something about work. Then I heard "Aunt Gertrude" and a chuckle, then something else I couldn't catch at all and then my dad was saying he forgot to mention it and my mom's voice was louder for a second. She sounded disappointed. A dog barked in another yard. I wondered if it was DaCostas'. Footsteps clicked along the street. My mom and dad called hi. I flipped my pillow over to the cool side, rolled over and it was morning.

I was up and dressed and downstairs before my

dad even called me. I ate my cereal so fast I could barely get my mouth shut. "The human vacuum cleaner." My dad shook his head. "You and your mother are running around like a couple of chickens with their heads off." I charged off to brush my teeth. "And take that tent," he called after me. "Your mom forgot the bikini this morning and I'm going to have to take the darn thing over to her school after I go shopping."

"Grbblmpfgh," I called around my toothbrush. No way was I going to forget Mr. Flynn's gift.

I turned off the tap and ran to the dining room. I grabbed a box, yelled goodbye, banged out the door and ran all the way down Greenapple Street. I didn't stop until I was in Room 7, where I hid the gift under a big box at the bottom of the coat racks. Alone in the classroom I imagined it all one more time: lemonade; trumpets; announcement; gift; everyone watching; cheers. Cyril the Hero. I wanted it to last forever.

When kids started coming in I led them back to peek under the box, but we left a lookout at the door in case Mr. Flynn came. Maggie was busy with the tape recorder and giving Monica instructions, so she didn't sneak a peek until just before the bell. I went back with her and tipped up the box. Even on the floor the present looked great, all shiny blue paper with a white bow.

"Beauties, huh?" I whispered, dropping the box back before Mr. Flynn noticed, but Maggie looked puzzled. Then she looked mixed up. Then she looked just plain mad.

"Cyril," she hissed. "You goon! We didn't use blue paper, we used green. That's not the tent, it's the bikini!" My stomach dropped half way to China. Unless somebody did something very smart very fast Mr. Flynn was going to get a leopard-skin bikini and I was going to get turned into hamburger by the rest of Room 7.

Somehow I got back to my desk. Okay, I told myself, okay. All you've got to do is … is … run away – no, is … is … *ask to phone home because you forgot something.* Of course. It was easy. It was even true. Maybe this genius stuff wasn't so hard after all.

As soon as announcements ended, I burned over to Mr. Flynn, got permission, and took off for the office. I'd call my dad, he'd bring over the tent and swap it for the bikini. Cinchy.

But it wasn't. I phoned three times and the line was busy. The secretary told me to come back later. No sweat, I told myself. There was lots of time. When I told Maggie, though, she didn't look happy.

"This could be trouble, Cyril," she warned. "You'd better keep me posted in case we need a plan."

"It'll be okay," I said, but now I wasn't sure.

"Maybe," Maggie scowled. "But you were dumb to mix them up in the first place."

"It wasn't my fault," I screeched, "my mom blew it."

"Hm," Maggie bunched her lips together. "You'd better phone again."

And I did. Again and again and again. The busy

signal made my whole stomach vibrate like jelly. Recess was coming up and time was running out. After recess Mr. Flynn was going to finish reading the book and then it was lemonade and the present.

Finally the line wasn't busy. I held on tight and got ready to talk really fast. There was nobody home.

It was like getting flattened by a steam roller. I could see it now: Mr. Flynn holding up a leopard-skin bikini, everybody screeching, me turning into a total bozo. Nobody would ever speak to me again. I wanted to hide in a waste basket until the caretaker took me away.

Then I saw Maggie at the door of the library. She had the riddle book in her hand, to take it back, I guess.

"So what happened?" As I told her, I started to get mad. After all, if my mom hadn't messed up and my dad hadn't gone out, everything would be fine. "Now it's all wrecked," I snarled.

"Oh, Cyril," Maggie snapped. "Phone your mom's school and leave a message for your dad to hurry up with the tent. We'll stall them."

"How?" I wailed. "It's almost recess."

"I don't know yet," said Maggie. "I'll think of something. But first I've got to take this back to the library and you have to phone. And Cyril," she warned as I turned to go, "you're going to ask your dad about Mrs. Hummaker when he gets here?"

"No sweat." It was easier than looking like a dwork with a leopard-skin bikini.

"*And –* "

"For sure," I promised, not even caring what it was. I was already running back to the office.

I got back to Room 7 before recess. Maggie came in just as the bell rang. "Hide in the washroom," she whispered, "and meet me back in here when everyone's gone out. I've got a plan."

When I slipped back into class Maggie was cutting out a piece of red construction paper. She barely looked up. "Mr. Flynn's on yard duty," she explained. "Stash these books in everybody's desks. I snuck them out of the library. When everyone finds them they'll all have to go back."

When I was done, Maggie told me to hide the lemonade cups somewhere; she put down her marker pen and folded the construction paper shut.

"I've got to go outside," she said. "Put the cookies in another cupboard or something, then take the card off the gift and get out of here."

"What are you doing?" I asked, fumbling with the stack of cups.

"Only the most importantly perfect part of the plan. So don't forget, after recess, no matter what, just do exactly what we planned last night." She was gone.

I stashed the cups and cookies in the wrong cupboards. Then, just to make sure, I moved half the social studies books we were collecting to the back of the coat closet and slipped the book Mr. Flynn was reading us to the very bottom of the papers on his desk. As the bell rang, I hid back in the washroom until everybody was going by. Maggie was almost the last in, carrying the construction paper, and ignoring me. I sank low in my seat and promised to be perfect forever if only this plan worked.

The promise didn't seem to help much. When Mr. Flynn called for the social studies books, loud-mouthed Bobby Devlin spotted them in the cupboard in about three seconds. Then the library books started turning up, and Mr. Flynn sent everybody to the library at once instead of one at a time. They got back so fast they must have ridden motorcycles. Then he bumped the papers on his desk and there was the book before he even looked for it. I couldn't believe it. Maggie just sat there as if everything was fine. Once she even yawned. I wanted to scream.

Mr. Flynn started to read, but I couldn't listen. I watched the hands creep around the face of the clock and sent out thought beams for my dad to show up. What was he doing, walking?

Before I knew it the story was over. Lemonade time. The cookies turned up as if Mr. Flynn had radar. There were still the cups, I thought. "No sense wasting time," he said and sent Monica next door to borrow some. My whole body turned to mashed potatoes.

I sat there in a lump as the lemonade got passed around, then the cookies. What were we going to do? I *hated* when Maggie didn't tell me stuff this way. Nobody *ever* told me stuff.

"Okay people," Mr. Flynn called, brushing up

his moustache like he always did when he had an announcement. "At eleven-thirty you'll be going to your new classrooms for a few minutes, so listen up for one last time. I hope you had a good time in Room 7 this year. I know I did.

"Next year at my new school I'm going to miss lots of people and lots of the things that happen around here." Mr. Flynn paused and looked around the room. Was I one of the ones he was going to miss? Not after he got that bikini. It wasn't fair. I was so mad my eyes got watery.

Mr. Flynn tugged at his moustache and went on. "I want to wish you all good luck and say I hope we'll meet again one of these days. But most of all may we all have a great summer!" Everybody cheered at that. Everybody but me, anyway. It was time for the gift.

Suddenly everyone was looking at me, then over at Maggie. I swallowed hard and looked at the floor. Stall, I thought, *stall.* Something clunked on a desk and *bammo!* the trumpet tape was blaring. My head snapped up so fast I nearly bounced off the ceiling. Monica was saying her stuff, and then everyone was looking at me again. Maggie had to be crazy. I jumped up and gargled the only thing I could think of:

"Can I go to the washroom?"

"Cyrilll," Monica hissed, "the present!"

Desperately I shook my head. "Not yet!" I mouthed back, but it was too late. Other kids were calling, "C'mon Cyril!" and Bobby Devlin was back at the closet yelling, "It's a present, sir, it's a present!" I stood there on my mashed-potato legs and watched Bobby parade it up to the front. And then the present was sitting on Mr. Flynn's desk and the whole class was surrounding him. The end of the world.

"What's this?" Mr. Flynn laughed. He was grinning so hard his moustache nearly stuck in his eyebrows.

From the very front of the crowd Russell said, "It's from all of us, sir." He put both hands on the present and pushed it a little towards Mr. Flynn.

"Aw, thank you, Russell, thank you, everybody." I wanted to laser-beam Russell into a little pile of dust.

"Open it," everyone cheered, "open it!" Mr. Flynn reached for the ribbon.

"Wait!"

Everything stopped. Maggie held up the folded red construction paper. "First you have to do the card."

Maggie barged through the crowd and handed Mr. Flynn the construction paper.

"Fair enough," said Mr. Flynn. He unfolded the paper and read out: "Guess this riddle and get a going away present."

Riddle, I thought, what riddle? Mr. Flynn read, "Why should you always take a baseball player camping with you?"

"No present till you guess." Maggie picked up the package and carried it back to my desk. I could feel my mouth hanging open.

"I have to guess?" said Mr. Flynn. He looked at the clock. "Wow, we haven't got much time."

"You can do it," Russell oozed. His voice was like hair gel. "Yeah, you can do it!" everybody called.

"Bet he can't," Maggie whispered to me. If he didn't guess by eleven-thirty, we'd have to wait till we got back from our new classes. My dad would have to be here by then. I started to hope again, just the tiniest micro-smallest bit.

"Why should...." Mr. Flynn looked at the floor, then at the ceiling, "why should ... *camping?*"

Somebody whispered. "NO HINTS!" Maggie ordered, like an army general. I held my breath.

"I know! Because they know how to get back to home base?"

"Nooooo," everyone groaned. I crossed my fingers.

"Because they can swat flies?"

"Nooooo!" I crossed my toes and shut my eyes.

"Because they're not afraid of bats?"

"NOOOO!" My stomach hung upside down. Mr. Flynn was twisting hard at his moustache now. His eyes went all narrow.

"Because ... Because. ..."

"MR. FLYNN?" the p.a. crackled overhead. Mr. Flynn called for quiet so he could hear. *"Would you send Cyril to the office please? His father is here."*

"Okay, thanks," called Mr. Flynn. "Cyril – "

I was half way out the door with the package before he even finished saying my name. Maggie didn't even blink. Behind me Mr. Flynn was saying, "Because they spend half their time in the field?"

"NOOOOO!" I had wheels now, boy.

I paid attention for about one second while my dad grumped about how my mom and I should get our acts together, then I was burning for Room 7 again. Cyril the Hero! I went into galaxydrive and skidded into Room 7 in time to hear " ... how to pitch a tent?"

"Right!" everyone was yelling at once. "Open it, sir, it's a tent!"

"Where is it?" Mr. Flynn called over the noise. Voices babbled. Heads turned to Maggie. Maggie turned to me.

"Here," I called. I charged up holding the present.

That's when I slipped on the cookie. "Awwp," I squawked and flopped across somebody's desk. The gift blooped out of my hands and just barely landed on Mr. Flynn's desk.

"Cyrilllll, quit hogging," Russell said. He passed the present to Mr. Flynn.

"Talk about special delivery," Mr. Flynn said. "You okay there, Cyril?"

It felt like I'd just hit a school bus with my stomach, but it beat having to eat a leopard-skin bikini. Mr. Flynn unwrapped the tent and everybody cheered.

"See, Cyril?" Maggie said. "Nothing to it."

Maggie and I walked home together at noon. At first I didn't feel so terrific. We'd gotten Mrs. Van

Loon for next year. Old Lady Loony everybody called her. She breathed fire even when she smiled. And then, after I got over sweating about the bikini I felt like I'd blown it with my tent plan. Oh, Mr. Flynn really liked the tent, but it didn't look like he'd be inviting me camping. Somehow I just looked like a klutzy messenger boy instead of the Greenapple Street Genius on a special mission for Mr. Flynn. After last bell I'd hung around Room 7 to say good-bye, but all these other kids were talking and getting his autograph, so finally I'd let Maggie drag me away.

But now, walking across the playground in the hot sun, it was all melting away. Old Lady Loony and the fall were a million years off. Mr. Flynn would find out about me and the tent, he had to. It was only fair. I'd make a plan with Maggie. Or maybe he'd just figure it out and call me up sometime. I'd bet he would. All at once I felt like I was zooming up giant-sized happy in the sunshine. It was *summer*. Anything could happen. Everything felt *more*. Suddenly I was starving. I jumped over the bike rack and yelled as loud as I could. Maggie laughed and yelled too. "Can't catch me!" I shouted and took off, and she couldn't, at least not till we were at the very edge of the playground.

"Hey, after lunch," I panted, "what do you want to do first?"

"First? First we're going to find out about your dad and Mrs. Hummaker."

"Aw," I groaned.

"Then we start a tent plan of our own. But very

first, I've got a riddle for you: what's gigantic and tough and you never know when it's going to hit you?"

"What?" I laughed.

"The favour you owe me for saving your bikini."

It didn't seem like much on the first day of summer.

The Yolk's on You

MY DAD WAS KIND OF MAD AT ME FOR messing up with the gifts but my mom had messed up too, and after a while he stopped griping about running a delivery service. Anyway, I was in trouble about other stuff by then, like when we went bananas with the car-wash hose or had the grape war on Leanne's patio while we were spying.

That stuff was Maggie's fault. She bossed a whole bunch of us into doing all kinds of junk to get money for a tent and keep an eye on Russell. Russell had his own gang too, that hung around the tree house and spied on us back. It was okay I guess, but after a while I wanted to quit. No way were we ever going to make enough money for a tent and I was getting tired of Maggie bossing us. Besides, Great Aunt Gertrude's visit was getting closer and closer and Maggie wasn't doing a thing about it. Every time I thought about it I felt more like a marshmallow.

And then, just in time, I got my own genius idea: the mystery letter. See, Maggie's tent stuff kept me remembering Mr. Flynn's gift and how Russell made it seem like he was in charge, even though he'd never paid a cent. If I let Mr. Flynn know it was me who thought up his tent, then he'd take me camping. Not only would that burn Russell, but if I worked fast I'd be leaving for camping just when Great Aunt Gertrude arrived. Perfect or what, huh?

I decided to tell Mr. Flynn by mystery letter. That's where you spell out the words with letters cut from newspapers and tape them on a page without signing any name. That way nobody knows who sent it because they can't tell the handwriting.

So on Tuesday morning, the second week of summer holidays, I snuck scissors, tape and a piece of paper down to the basement where we keep papers and magazines. This plan was so secret that not even Maggie was going to know. A lot of jaws were going to hit the floor when Mr. Flynn called up, boy.

I pulled the practice copy of my letter out of my sock and smoothed it out. It read:

Dere Mr. Flynn

Gess who told everybody get you a tent?

Cyril did. He loves camping.

A freind.

P.S. Russell never pade.

Perfect, I thought, and got started. It was nice working by myself in the basement. Outside it was already hot but down here it was cool and dim, like under water. Would Mr. Flynn take me scuba diving when we camped ... maybe we'd have to wrestle an octopus. I shook my head. This was work time. I started cutting letters and listening to my mom talking on the phone in the kitchen. As long as she was doing that she couldn't snoop on what I was doing. Besides, you never knew when grownups were going to talk about you.

It was only ten after nine and it was her second phone call. Somebody had called about two minutes ago and now she was calling my dad at the newspaper. Someone had cancelled, she was saying " ... No, we have to decide right away. C'mon, Arch, it'll be fun ... yes, it's when Gertrude's coming, but I'll call her right now. She'd love to ... Okay, 'bye."

What was that about Great Aunt Gertrude? I heard my mom dialling the phone again and I put down the scissors. Maybe I should listen to this more carefully.

"Aunt Gertrude? It's Jan here. How are you? ... Well, Auntie Gert, that's why I'm calling. You see there's – " BANG BANG BANG!

I nearly swallowed my socks. My mom stopped talking. Her footsteps thumped along the hall above me. There were voices. "Cyril," she called, "it's for you."

I got to the hall as my mom picked up the phone again. Maggie and Monica were standing at the front door. My mom started to talk but before I could listen, Monica squealed, "Hurry up, Cyril. You have to come with us."

"What?" I said, still trying to hear my mom. "Wait!"

"Uh-uh, this is it, Cyril. The greatest thing to

33

happen all summer and we need everybody. Look!" Maggie dragged me out the door and pointed while Monica babbled how great it was. Down the street I saw a big yellow truck stopped at the Vulkoviches' house. Men were unloading two giant boxes, a tall one and a square one.

"So what?" I squirmed, leaning back to the door screen. Inside my mom was laughing and saying she hoped something but I couldn't tell what, Monica was making so much noise.

"It's a fridge and stove," she squawked. "A fridge and stove."

"What?" I said.

"Terrific," came my mom. "That's what – "

"Maybe a freezer but for sure a stove."

"Oh, I know, Auntie Gert!"

"When we got a stove – "

If my ears had to stretch any farther, they'd look like an elephant's. My brain felt like a ping-pong ball. Maggie hauled me to the steps. "Let's go."

"*Huuuuh?* Where?" I tried to step back.

"To get those boxes, silly. For a clubhouse in my back yard. Russell is doomed!"

"I – I – have to ask first!" I sputtered. "I – 'cause I was doing some stuff."

"Okay, but *move it.* Meet us over there." Maggie and Monica ran for their bikes and took off.

I had to go – but at least I could hear the rest of the phone call. I whipped back in the house. My mom was still talking but now she was asking someone for my dad again. I clomped down to the basement and hid my letter stuff, then went back to the kitchen, listening. There was nothing to hear. My mom was still waiting. So much for important telephone stuff.

I asked could I go and she said yes, but I had to take the garbage down to the street first.

When I got done, Maggie and Monica were standing by their bikes at the end of Vulkoviches' drive. Men were hauling a box up the front steps.

By the time I got over there, the men were in the house. Maggie had barged right up the steps and was knocking and peering inside. Mrs. Vulkovich answered. She was a big, white-haired lady who was nice unless you cut across her lawn. Right now she looked red in the face, like she was in a hurry. I could hear grunting and screeching noises as the men moved things in the kitchen. The phone was ringing, too. Maggie asked for the boxes politely, but you could tell she was all excited.

"Sure, sure, Maggie, you can have them." Mrs. Vulkovich kept looking over her shoulder as she talked. It sounded like they had a bulldozer in there. Mr. V. was yelling, "Ya, ya, sure," into the phone.

"Come back in an hour, dear," said Mrs. V.

"Yes, ma'am. Thank you," Maggie said politely, grinning so hard I thought her teeth would crack. "Now," she said as we all went down the steps, "we get everybody and meet at my place."

Fifty-nine and a half minutes later we were heading up Greenapple Street. Lester and Karina had their wagons and everyone had left their bikes at my place so they could help. Even I was starting to feel excited. Maggie made the clubhouse sound so good it was hard not to run.

The truck was gone and the boxes were standing at the end of Vulkoviches' driveway near the street. They were fantastic – huge, made from wood and thick cardboard, with big printing all over them. You could fit all of us in easy. George said, "Look at this. Put this one up for a lookout tower."

"No, make it a tunnel," shouted Monica. "And this for the main room."

"And let's cut windows."

"And make a flag."

"And dig a secret passage underground to a trap door!"

"And have 'Keep Out' signs and a password!"

"Oh yeah!"

"Ever beauties!"

"Awesome, man!"

Lester's dad had some paint we could have. Karina could get a hammer and nails. I had a flag. Maggie said this was even better than a tree house because we could change it around any way we wanted, all the time. Everybody's brain was bubbling over. Then George said, "Uh-oh. What do they want?"

We looked. Russell and Tracey and Bobby and the rest of them were coming down the street. They were glaring at us. Maggie said, "Who cares?" and moved over to the tall carton.

"DON'T TOUCH THOSE BOXES!" Russell

shouted and *whammo* they were all charging towards us.

"Those are MINE," Russell panted. He could sound like a jerkface even when he was out of breath.

Maggie said, "Get lost, Russell. I already asked Mrs. V. for them."

"Yeah? Well, I phoned and asked Mr. Vulkovich an hour ago and he said *I* could have them."

Monica turned and looked at me. We were both remembering Mr. V. shouting into the telephone. Maggie just glared back at Russell and snapped, "Let's go find out."

Russell shrugged. "It's your funeral." The rest of us waited on the walk while they climbed the steps.

The Vulkoviches were pretty embarrassed. "Now why not choose one box each?" Mr. Vulkovich smiled. "Then everyone is happy. Okay kids? Bye-bye."

But everyone wasn't happy. One box was bigger than the other and you'd need both to make anything really neat.

"I guess we'll have to fight it out," said Maggie.

Heads jerked around. A fight? "We'll have a duel, a duel for the boxes."

Russell snorted. "What with, swords?"

"Just pound her," said Bobby.

"Try it, Bobby," Maggie warned. Bobby stuck out his tongue, but he stepped back. Maggie was bigger than he was. "No pounding. Just eggs."

"Eggs?" said a bunch of us.

"Egg toss?" Russell asked carefully. "Like at field day?"

"Right." And then I understood. I wished I hadn't. Just the thought of an egg toss made me feel as if I'd sat on a cold pizza. You played against another team, tossing an egg back and forth with your partner until one team broke their egg. Every time you made a catch, you both took a step back so the next throw was longer. On field day, I'd been partners with Karina and we'd played against Maggie and Russell. It was the only time Maggie and Russell teamed up in their whole lives. They didn't want to, but a teacher picked the teams. All day long they bugged each other, but they also cleaned up in everything. The only thing I cleaned up was me, after Karina threw our egg a little too hard and a little too high. I could still feel the goo oozing through my fingers, splattering down my head and dripping down my neck, the crackle of the shell in my hands. Egg shampoo. Disgustingly sick.

Maggie was grinning. "Winner gets the boxes. You and Bobby against me and – " she jerked her head back " – Cyril."

"What?" I yelled.

"Right after lunch."

"Why not now?" Lester asked.

"You shut up!" I screeched.

Russell didn't say anything for a long time. Then he smiled like a vampire. "Okay, but we do it in my back yard. And nobody touches the boxes till after."

Maggie said no sweat and marched us back to my

garage like we were an army. Everyone was calling out about who was going to get fried or scrambled, but I felt squishy already.

We sat in my garage and kept an eye on Russell and the boxes. Naturally motormouth Monica had to start yakking about how egg sandwiches were her favourite and how her dad once dropped a whole carton of eggs in the kitchen and the dog got in them. I wanted to stuff my head in the lawn-mower bag to keep from hearing. Maggie just sat there like she was dreaming.

After a while, Lester said, "Hey, aren't you guys going to practise or anything?"

"We don't have to," Maggie said, and smiled her most incredibly secret-type smile. "I've got a plan."

"What is it?" I almost shouted.

Maggie rolled her eyes. "What's Monica been talking about?"

"Egg sandwiches," we all said.

"And how do you get eggs ready for egg sandwiches?"

Who knows? I hate egg sandwiches. But George said, "You hard boil them."

"Uh-huh," said Maggie. "And what do hardboiled eggs look like before you take off the shells?"

"*I get it,*" we all yelled at once, and Karina shouted, "You're going to use a hard-boiled egg so it won't break!"

Maggie smiled that smile again and shook her head. "Better than that. Everybody was talking about that back at field day, remember? Russell will bring a hard-boiled egg. He's not a complete dim bulb. So we're going to take a *raw* egg and – "

"Say you want to swap eggs to be fair!" Monica grinned.

"Right." Maggie looked a little bugged that Monica figured it out. "That way we get their hard-boiled one. It'll serve them right, the dirty cheaters."

"All right!" Everybody started slapping hands and shaking their fists in the air. Lester did a little dance like he'd just scored a goal. I took a deep breath and hoped that it would work. Some of Maggie's plans didn't always go exactly the way she said. She was going to owe me for this one.

After everyone else left for lunch, I said, "So if I help with this, you owe me back, right?"

"Cyrilllll. No way. Who owes me for saving him from giving Mr. Flynn a bikini, huh? You still owe *me*."

"Get out." I couldn't believe it. "This is extra special, for your clubhouse. *You* owe me!"

Maggie put her hands on her hips. "I'm doing this for you too, you know. See," Maggie whispered, "if we have a clubhouse and you helped get it maybe you could stay there when your Great Aunt Gertrude comes."

I'd never thought of that. It made sense. I mean what if Mr. Flynn could only take me camping part of the time Great Aunt Gertrude was here? A clubhouse would really come in handy.

"*If* you help with this perfectly safe completely positively hard-boiled egg plan," Maggie said, as if she were reading my mind. "I'll just call it a favour and you won't even owe me. Okay, partner?"

"Well. . . . " It *was* an easy plan, catching a hard-boiled egg. I pushed the words "egg shampoo" out of my mind and said, "Okay."

"Excellent," Maggie whooped. "Just do what I say and this will be fantastic. See you after lunch," and she took off through the back yards for home.

I whipped through my sandwiches as fast as I could, then took my orange downstairs so I could work on the letter for a little bit. I got as far as:

dERe mR FlYnn

gEsS WHO tOL

before it was time to go outside.

Lester was first to show up, hopping over the garbage bags and cans along the street. Maggie was last. She brought an egg.

"Good thing it's garbage day," she said. "This one's rotten."

The sky had clouded over at lunch time and Greenapple Street looked tired and gloomy. It was so hot that little tar bubbles were all over the road. The way they stuck to my runners made me feel sticky, even inside. Nobody talked. We were like cowboys walking along Main Street for the show-down. Maybe it would rain before the shooting started.

Up Russell's drive we went, past the garage and behind the hedge. Things had changed in Maggie's old back yard. Now there were these polka-dotted pretend mushrooms scattered on the grass and statues of gnomes and elves and a fake deer with a flower pot in its back. It was pretty amazing. Russell and the others were sitting under the tree, as if they were gnomes, too. Above them was Maggie's old tree house. I must have climbed up there a million times before Maggie moved.

We all came to the centre of the yard. Russell and Bobby and Maggie and me were right in the middle.

"Ready?" Russell asked.

"Of course," said Maggie. She slowly held up our egg. Somebody giggled. Russell carefully took his out of his shirt pocket, way too carefully, I thought, like he was faking something. I felt a little better.

Then they both said, "Let's trade."

Everyone froze. Russell said, "You *want* to trade?"

Maggie said, "*You* want to trade?"

I didn't need to say anything. Maggie and Russell had outsmarted each other. Now it was fair and square. With rotten eggs. I swallowed hard, and started to edge backwards but I bumped into someone. There was no way out.

"Aw, let's just do it," snorted Russell.

We shuffled into place, me facing Maggie, Bobby facing Russell. "Throw at the same time, remember," Maggie ordered, "and everybody steps back one foot every time."

"Okay, okay," Bobby whined. From the distance came a rumbling like thunder. I took a deep breath.

"Ready," said Maggie. "Go."

It was easy for the first five seconds. Then it was like walking a tightrope in skates. You'd watch the throw, slow and gentle, everyone holding their breath as the egg sailed towards you, getting faster somehow as it got closer and then it would plop! smooth and wobbly into your hands. Then everybody would cheer and you'd remember to breathe again as you tried to make your step back tiny without getting caught. Then would come the quiet again as everyone waited for the next throw, and in the distance that rumbling, getting louder all the time.

Farther and farther apart we moved until no one dared to breathe. Sweat prickled around my eyes. My hands felt slippery. "Not so hard!" I cried to Maggie after a tough throw. "I can't help it," she shot back. Russell and Bobby were snapping at each other, too. Somebody was going to miss soon.

Bobby and I threw back to Russell and Maggie. We all took another step back. I looked over at Maggie and wiped my hands hard on my shorts. It was getting darker all the time. The rumbling was louder, with booms and screeches and clatters. Bobby and I got set. They were so far away it looked like the throw was coming from the next block. Maggie pressed her lips together. Russell bit down on his tongue. They leaned and threw, and the eggs were lofting towards us end over end, up, then down, coming fast. We shuffled our feet, knees bent, hands out, fingers open, getting ready, here it came, any second, and BA-ROOOOOOMM! a tremendous roar exploded from the street. Something hollow clattered and boomed on the pavement and

Bobby and I were covered with rotten egg.

An incredible stink filled the back yard. Everybody started shouting at once. Except me. I didn't want to get egg in my mouth. Bobby was down on his knees yelling "Gross!" and trying to wipe his face with his arm and wipe his hands on the grass at the same time. I just stood there and dripped.

"A tie!"

"No way, Cyril first!"

"Bobby, it was Bobby!"

The rumbling was still there, but going away now. Was it thunder? There wasn't one drop of rain. Then it was as if a spell had been broken.

"Ohmygosh," Monica screamed, "the garbage truck!"

It was just turning the corner as we got to the street. Except for a car and some empty garbage tins, Greenapple Street was empty. The boxes were gone.

"Ohhh, no!" Bobby yelled. Everybody was groaning. Russell and Maggie looked as if they just flunked a test.

We all wandered into the back yard again, moaning and grumbling. Bobby sat down on one of the polka-dot mushrooms and it fell over.

"Watch it!" Russell growled. He kicked at a gnome and missed.

"Whadda we do now?" somebody asked.

"Aw, who cares?" Tracey said. "I'm going to camp anyway, day after tomorrow."

"Yeah, me too," said Monica. Russell said he was

going to his cottage and then to camp, so he didn't care.

"Anybody wanna go skateboarding at the school?" Lester asked.

"Hey, yeah!" He and Bobby and George headed off together. Leanne and Karina wandered away to run through Leanne's sprinkler. Monica and Tracey decided to go to the store. Maggie and I started back down Greenapple Street. Did I ever stink. I sighed and rubbed my face against the shoulder of my shirt. My hands were all crackly and sticky where the egg had dried. I stuffed them in my pockets to wipe them and looked at Maggie as she slouched along.

I said, "At least Russell's going away for a while." Maggie didn't answer.

A drop of rain plopped on my head as we got to my driveway.

"See ya," Maggie sighed. She was taking the long way home, even in the rain.

It cleared up by supper time. I'd told my mom we'd had a baking accident with the egg and she stuck me in the shower. Then I'd done some more on my letter until I ran out of tape. Now that there was no clubhouse, the letter was super important again. Great Aunt Gertrude's visit was pretty soon. Somehow Maggie's plan getting wrecked had made me nervous all over again.

So at supper, when my mom said she had good news for me, I sure was ready.

"Cyril, we're renting a cottage for the next two

weeks. It's just outside Grandville, right on the lake."

"Wow," I shouted, and almost lost some pork chop. "Fworry." I closed my mouth and chewed like crazy.

"We're renting it through Russell's mother. She told your dad about it ages ago."

"The classic hard sell," my dad snorted. "She did everything but pin me down on the hood of her car. It's a good thing I wasn't dressed for success, or she would have ruined my suit."

I stared at my dad. What was he talking about?

"Oh, for heaven's sake, Arch," my mom said. "All she did was give you her card, and you forgot all about it."

"Gave me her card, threw me over the car, what's the difference?"

"Now Archie, she only called again this morning because a cottage came available. Be fair. It's nice we got another chance."

My mind was bouncing all over the place. So that's why Russell's mom called to my dad.

"I thought maybe she was trying to sell you a swamp," I thought out loud.

"Maybe that's where the cottage is," said my dad.

My mom laughed and shook her head. "Now, now, it won't be that bad. Easier than camping, I guarantee." She winked at me. "Even for a city boy."

"What isn't?" my dad said. "I'm not much of a cottager either."

"But you promised you'd enjoy it, right?" my mom said.

46

"Well, I can take some file stuff to work on for the paper."

"*Right?*" my mom said again.

"Right," said my dad. "I'll just pretend I'm Mr. Flynn."

That stopped me for a second. Had I been talking about Mr. Flynn a lot? The thought of a cottage made me too excited to care much. Then I remembered. "What about Great Aunt Gertrude?"

"Oh, she's coming, too," my mom said. "She was so excited on the phone this morning. Like old times, she said, absolutely wonderful."

"Oh." It didn't sound so wonderful to me.

"But," said my mom, "since I'm bringing a guest, you can, too. You can invite Maggie if you want – AFTER dinner." I was already jumping up.

"Hey, what about me? Can't I bring somebody?" My dad pretended he was going to cry.

"Nooo, dear, not this time." My mom talked like you do to babies. "You already have enough of us to cook for."

My dad got all droopy. Then he straightened up. "*Well.* Bread and water every night then." He wiggled his eyebrows.

Right after supper I called Maggie. "Remember what you wanted to know about my dad? Well, the Greenapple Street Genius has found out!"

She nearly bonged off the ceiling when I told her all the news. Her parents said yes so Maggie came over on her bike and we zoomed around the neighbourhood. We wanted to tell the whole world, but the only person we saw was Russell. He was out pegging an old tennis ball at his garage door. We screeched up to his driveway and I called, "Ha ha, Russell, we're going away too!"

"Big deal. My mom already told me. Anyway you got a crummy cottage. Mine is way better. *And* you're not exactly the only ones in the world renting a cottage, you know." He said that part with his know-it-all nose way up in the air. Planes could have flown in his nostrils.

"How do you know it's crummy, anyway? It's far away from here."

That vampire grin on his face again sent a little prickle down my spine. "Because," he said, "my cottage is three doors away, that's why."

It was like the egg toss all over again. I squinched so hard my chin almost hit my nose.

Russell pegged the ball. It thumped off the door. "I'm going to be there. So don't forget, it's my place." *Thump.* "I'm the one who does stuff." *Thump.* "If you don't bug me too much – " *thump* "– I might even show you some neat things." *Thump.* "Maybe." *Thump.* He never even looked around from the door. At least he didn't see the face I made.

Maggie pushed off on her bike. "Don't worry," she said as we rolled off, "I'll think of something."

I already had. With Great Aunt Gertrude coming and Russell there, too, I'd have to finish that letter before it was too late.

Smarter than You Sink

WHEN THE CAR FINALLY STOPPED, Great Aunt Gertrude was first one out. She whooshed out a breath, stretched her arms and bounced on her toes.

"Come on, kiddos," she cried in her dry, raspy voice, "you've been sitting too long."

The bright stripes of her tennis shirt bobbed up and down and the ends of her ears joggled in time. She really did have the longest ear lobes in the world – not down to her shoulders or anything, but long. When Maggie first saw them she started to whisper that song,

Do your ears hang low,
Do they wobble to and fro?

and I nearly sprayed my pop all over Greenapple Street. Great Aunt Gertrude didn't notice; like always, she was too busy talking. Maybe that's why her voice was so scratchy.

Now, though, I closed my eyes. Watching jiggling ear lobes was making me a little car sick again.

Maggie scrambled out of the back seat, where I had been squished between her and my mom.

"Come on, Maggie," Great Aunt Gertrude croaked, "last one in is a rotten egg."

"In what?" Maggie was asking as they moved off.

"The lake, sweetie, the lake. Let's get some sand in your shoes."

I climbed out of the car as they went skipping past the trees to the bright green lawn of the cottage. Past it was a flash of blue. The lake? I took a deep breath and raced to catch up.

Already I wasn't doing so hot with Great Aunt Gertrude. At dinner the night before, I'd tried to skip my zucchini and she caught me. I got told I needed some flesh on my bones *and* to speak up and stop mumbling *and* to go out and get some exercise after dinner instead of reading. Talk about bossy, it was like having Maggie for your grandma, only worse.

Not that Great Aunt Gertrude looked much like a grandma, even though she was one. I mean she looked pretty old, but not little-old-lady old, and not all dressed up like I thought she'd be. She had curly yellow hair and a tan and she wore shorts and tennis shirts and a diving watch and shaded wire glasses. For a grownup she was pretty short, and kind of round and comfortable looking. But she moved fast and she could give you this X-ray eye that made you feel like a marshmallow. I had a scary feeling she might surprise you if you arm wrestled with her. And you never knew what she was going to do next. It made me very glad I'd brought along my mystery letter to Mr. Flynn. I'd decided to give cottaging a chance but if things didn't go okay I'd finish the letter real fast, mail it, and then Mr. Flynn would come and take me away camping.

I zoomed out from the trees past the cottage towards the beach and the lake. It was so fantastic I forgot all about Great Aunt Gertrude. The breeze was blowing and everything smelled all watery. If you looked straight out there was blue almost as far as you could see, all ripply and sparkling so it hurt your eyes. There were sailboats too, where the water turned purple, so small they looked like bathtub toys. I was squinting so hard that I almost didn't see the edge of the lawn. It was a high bank that dropped away to the beach.

"The stairs, Cyril. Use the stairs." Maggie and Great Aunt Gertrude were on the beach, pointing to my left. I bombed along the bank to where it turned in at some trees and found these rickety wooden steps with a rusty pipe railing. About one second later I was down by the water, pulling off my shoes and socks. Aunt Gertrude and Maggie were already wading.

"Is it cold?" I asked, flubbing with my shoe-lace.

"It's just right," said Maggie, "but it's all rocks on the bottom."

"Not out here it isn't," called Great Aunt Gertrude from a little farther out. "It turns to sand."

I poked a foot in. The water slipped between my toes and lapped at my ankles. It was perfect. The stones felt slippery and mysterious. Up close the water was clear where it was shallow and shady

51

green where it got deeper. "All right," I breathed.

"You're darn tootin'." Great Aunt Gertrude sloshed back in. "I'm for a swim. But first we've got to get unpacked. Come on, slowpokes, or they'll think we've drowned." She marched to the steps.

I grabbed for my shoes, behind again. When I caught up to Maggie she grinned. "Your Great Aunt Gertrude is really nice. She's funny."

"I guess," I said. I was about to say, "But she doesn't pick on you," when Maggie poked me. "Oh-oh," she whispered. "The enemy."

Three cottages away Russell was standing on the lawn. It sloped right down to the beach at his place. Then something unbelievable happened: Maggie waved. Russell lifted his hand so slowly it must have weighed three hundred pounds. When it got to his waist it flopped back down again. That was his wave back.

I whipped around to Maggie. "What'd you *wave* for?"

"It's my new plan." She kept her voice low. "Russell said be nice to him and he'd show us stuff, remember? Well, we're going to be nice to the little toad – until he shows me something I can ransom for my tree house."

"*What?*" I made my ripple potato chip face. Maggie had to be dreaming. No way was Russell going to give up that tree house. "That's gross," I said. "I'm not being nice to him."

"Cyrilllllll," said Maggie. "It'll be easy." She didn't sound very convincing. I thought again about my mystery letter. Before I could say anything more we were climbing the steps and then it was cottage time.

Well, no matter what Russell said, the cottage wasn't crummy. It was made of wood painted white and green with a screened porch. The front door was open and my dad was carrying stuff down from the car. I hurried inside. There it was all wood too, only not painted. You could see right up into the roof and the floor creaked like anything when you walked on it. It was all warm from being shut up, and goldy-coloured from the sun shining through the yellow curtains. In the warmth the cottage smelled like a closed-up forest full of wood, dust, smoke, old magazines and a million other things that I didn't know what they were yet. Great Aunt Gertrude started pulling back the curtains and opening windows and the watery lake smell came in too.

In the living-room, there was a fireplace made of stones all cemented together and big, faded, saggy old chairs and couch that I bounced on, just to test them.

At the back on one side was a little tiny kitchen. My mom was poking around in the cupboards and unloading stuff from the food hamper. On the other side was an even teenier bathroom. My dad peered in. "Well, it's better than an outhouse." I heard him sigh, but we were already checking out the bedrooms. There were three of them in a row down one side of the place.

The front one had one big bed and the other two

had bunks. Great Aunt Gertrude said my mom and dad got the first room, I got the middle and Maggie got the back.

"Where will you sleep?" Maggie wanted to know.

"On the porch in the fresh air. Didn't you see that sleeping couch at the far end? The porch bed is the best one at a cottage. That's why it's for me, heh, heh, heh. Now get those bags into your rooms. Scoot!" Great Aunt Gertrude waved her arms at us.

I went in my room and dumped my backpack on the bottom bunk. "Pssst! Cyril!" I looked around. Maggie was whispering to me from somewhere. "Up top!" I climbed to the top bunk. There was a crack in the boards where I could hear perfectly. We could talk and plan stuff even after bedtime. It was excellent.

"Shake a leg, you two," called Great Aunt Gertrude, "there's work to do."

By the time we got the car unpacked it was time for lunch. My mom and Great Aunt Gertrude made sandwiches and we sat at a big green table on the front porch.

"Is this where we eat all the time?" I asked.

"Unless we're out at the picnic table," my mom said. "There's no room in the kitchen and your dad's going to be barbecuing all the time anyway. Right dear?" She looked at my dad.

"Absolutely," he said, "as long as you all do the fishing and hunting."

I stared. Was he kidding or what? Then my mom

said, "After lunch, some of us will go on an expedition to town and do some hunting in the supermarket."

That made me feel better. For a second there I'd had a picture of Great Aunt Gertrude wrestling a moose and then making *me* wrestle the second one.

Next we got "The Law of the Lake." It was like being back in kindergarten.

"All right," Great Aunt Gertrude rasped. "Remember Rules for Water Rats, Jan? You tell 'em."

"Number one," said my mom, "is Never Swim Alone. Two: Don't Go in the Water Without Permission. Three is Always Wear a Life-Jacket in a Boat."

"Darn right," said Great Aunt Gertrude. "Number four: Always Tell Somebody Where You're Going." She stared at us over her dark glasses. My mom said, "Number five is Don't Track Sand Into the Cottage. Number six – " she looked at Great Aunt Gertrude, who said, "Wet Towels and Bathing Suits Get Hung Outside Right Away. The line's out back. Use it!"

My mom nodded and they sat there looking like Maggie did when she'd just shown how smart she was and how dumb you were.

"Rule number seven," my dad said, "Arch gets to be a beach bum instead of cooking."

We all groaned. Great Aunt Gertrude growled, "Beach bum, my eye, a city boy like you. We're going to get you hiking and swimming."

"Forget swimming," my dad said. "Floating's my game. We'll need Sayings for the Soggy."

Maggie and I giggled.

"Don't listen to him, you two," my mom warned. "This is serious business. We don't want anyone lost or drowned or making work for others. Just remember." She went over the Water Rat Rules again. "And," she said, "there's one more. I want you to invite Russell to play."

"What?" I screeched.

"You heard me," said my mom. "His brother's at camp and he's all alone up here."

"What about his mom and dad?" I said.

"You know what I mean. No fooling now. You go on over after lunch."

I groaned. Great Aunt Gertrude reminded me that lunch included eating my radishes.

Well, my mom didn't say *when* after lunch, so I thought maybe we should do about eight thousand other things first.

"We'd better go now," Maggie said, and looked at her watch. "Your mom said we'd go swimming at two-thirty, so it's only an hour and a half."

"Only?"

"Remember my plan, Cyril. A rat like Russell might take a lot of being nice to before he breaks down and I cream him. Come on." She started for Russell's place.

"This is disgusting," I sighed, but I followed her.

At first it wasn't that disgusting. Not pukey disgusting anyway. Oh, Russell was as jerky as ever and Maggie was yuckily, grossly sweet to him, but there was so much to see and do that I didn't pay much attention.

We headed up the beach. It curved past the cottages to a place where willow trees were tumbling down into the sand. There was all kinds of stuff washed up along the shore with the driftwood. Maggie found a shoe and some yellow rope. I found an empty bottle with the cap on. We set it up on a log and threw stones at it but nobody could hit it so we threw it back in the water to see where it would land. Then Russell found a tall plastic bucket with a wire handle. It wasn't even cracked.

Underneath the willow trees was a pond. A stream from it ran out into the lake. We scrambled around in the trees bashing at dead branches, and then we found sticks that looked like guns and played war for a while. It was great, except Russell would never die. He said we always just winged him. Sucky baby, I thought, but Maggie didn't say a word.

Finally we sat down on a log by the pond. I plunked a pebble into the middle and watched the ripples spread.

"It's bottomless." Russell nodded at the pond. "And you know what else? It's supposed to be haunted from some guy who got drown-ded."

"Drowned." Maggie always corrected people, even when she was being nice. I didn't care how he said it, it was weird.

"Really?" I said. I looked from the twisted shapes of the trees and the flickering shadows of their leaves down into the silent pond. Something fluttered on the back of my neck and I jumped.

Russell laughed and took his hand away. "Sucker," he said. Maggie rolled her eyes and smiled. I got up and went into the sunshine where the water streamed into the lake. "Ha, ha," I sneered to myself. Being nice to Russell didn't mean Maggie had to laugh at me. I ground the stones with my shoes. At my feet the stream was shallow and rushing. Looking into it I saw a beautiful stone. It was pure white and all round and smooth. I lifted it out of the water and little sparkly bits flashed. Feeling better, I put it in my pocket.

We headed back along the beach having contests. Maggie could throw a stone farthest out into the lake. Russell skipped one the most times. I came last more than anybody else. I know because Russell kept count. In fact he jumped up on a log and told the whole world. I was steaming, but Maggie just shook her head and hissed, "Don't forget my plan, Cyril." As soon as Russell wasn't looking, though, I jumped up on the log, stuck my nose up in the air, made my ripple chip face again and pretended to be Russell saying how great he was. It made me feel a lot better. After that I watched the water for neat stones and let the other two play.

When we got back to the cottage, it was swimming time. I thought we'd be rid of Russell but my mom invited him to swim with us and he went to get into his suit.

"Don't worry," Maggie said as we headed for the

cottage. "Maybe he can't swim very well. We'll have to save him from drowning and he'll owe us the tree house."

But he could swim just fine. In fact Russell could swim, brag and be sucky to grownups all at the same time. Disgusting plus. We heard about his mom selling a house for a million dollars once and his brother getting every Boy Scout badge and his dad having the greatest camera in the universe. I watched my dad floating on his back like a waterlogged tree and wished he'd do something great to shut Russell up. Instead he went back to the beach and lay down on a towel.

"Your dad doesn't swim very well, does he?" said Russell.

"He runs," I said. "Ten miles. Every day. Fast." My dad didn't go that far and he didn't go every day, but Russell didn't have to know.

Russell said, "Swimming's better. He doesn't have a tan, either."

"Too busy," I said. "He's thinking about the next book he's going to write. He's thinking right now, even." We looked. My dad's eyes were closed. "See?"

Russell didn't look convinced, so I was glad when Maggie challenged him to a breath-holding contest under water. I waded back to where it was shallower and found a beautiful black and white stone and a pebble with red and white and gold and green running through it. I saved them. I really wanted something that would make Russell clam up. The only problem was, except for gluing his mouth shut, I couldn't think of a thing. Finally, my mom and Great Aunt Gertrude got him. They could turn somersaults under water and dared us to try. We all got enough water up our noses to float an aircraft carrier.

Great Aunt Gertrude dove for another somersault, then popped up and stuck out her tongue. "Remind me to show you how one day," she said, and headed in. My mom went for a longer swim. Maggie wanted to try somersaults again but Russell had another idea: make a diving helmet. "We can use that bucket," he said. "It'll be perfect."

Diving! Even I got excited. That was Mr. Flynn stuff. I didn't care if it was Russell's idea, I beat them both to shore.

After that I was a total nerdoid, at least that's what Russell called me. Every time I made a suggestion he'd say, "Cyril, just let a real brain handle this, okay?" with this look on his face that said if I was lucky I could kiss his toes later. I was ready to murder him with the stupid bucket, especially after he did stuff I'd thought up but pretended it was his idea.

He didn't do that with Maggie, boy. I mean, he teased her a little but mainly they kept giving each other better ideas, saying "Yeah! And then you could … " all buddy-buddies. Maybe you had to get Russell a little scared of you or do great with him at field day or something before you were allowed to talk.

So they sat there at Russell's picnic table making

all the plans and doing the good parts and ordering me around like a slave. I'll show them, I thought. Just wait till the exact right moment when they get stuck and then I'll do something geniusy.

When the helmet was done, we took it down to the beach. Nobody else was there, except my dad down by our place. He was still thinking or snoozing, only now he was pinker.

"Okay," Russell said, "time for the big test." What they'd done was pretty neat. The bucket was upside down so it fit over your head. There was a hole in the side taped over with plastic kitchen wrap so you could see out. At the top of the helmet was another hole with one end of a garden hose stuck into it. The other end of the hose was attached to Russell's bicycle pump. That was for the air.

There was only one thing I didn't get: why wouldn't the water just fill up the helmet from its open end? Russell sighed. "Watch, dumb one." He stuck the helmet straight down in the water, open end first. It bobbed back up under his hands.

"There's air trapped underneath, Cyril," Maggie explained. "It keeps the water out."

"And if you two keep pumping," said Russell, "there'll be lots of air. So let's go." He lifted the helmet out of the water and stuck it on his head.

"Stahd umpfuhn," he yelled from inside the bucket. I looked at Maggie. "Start pumping, I guess," she said, and picked up the bicycle pump. "You keep the hose straight."

We watched Russell creep out into deeper water,

almost to his stomach. He stood teetering on the stones, out where the water turned dark and mysterious. Then all of a sudden he was shuffling back to shore like a shark was after him.

"I, uh, want to get my beach shoes," he explained in this squirmy voice after he took off the helmet. He made a face and waggled one foot in the air.

It *was* hard walking barefoot but it didn't look *that* tough.

"What's the matter, Russell?" I laughed. "Scared you'll have to run away from something?"

"No way," Russell said, as if he was daring me to fight. Right then I didn't even care about that. I didn't care about Maggie hissing at me either, it felt so good to pick on Russell.

"Yes, you are!" I shouted. "You're chicken of the underwater bogeyman!" I wiggled my fingers at him and laughed like a maniac. "Russell is a chicken! Russell is a chicken!" So much for be-nice-to-Russell plans. This was more like it. Russell was snarling and sputtering all over the place about how he wasn't scared of anything.

"Like fun," I said. And then I saw my genius chance. "Want me to do it for you, little Russy-wussy baby?" I crossed my toes and hoped.

Russell glared at me, then at the water. Really fast he said, "Okay, Cyril, if you're such a big hero, go first. See if I care."

"Okay, I will. Start pumping." I snatched the helmet from him and stuck it on my head. Who cared if Russell was steamed at me, so what if Maggie looked like she wanted to send me to Pluto? It was time for me to be a star.

I shuffled into the water. The wire handle of the bucket flopped against my chest and I smelled a lot of plastic.

From far away came a tiny hissing noise: the air pump. I held the bucket down on my shoulders with both hands and went deeper into the water. The hose dragged the top of the bucket backwards, so my forehead stuck to the plastic wrap and all I could see was bucket. The bottom of the lake seemed even rockier in front of Russell's cottage. Maybe Russell wasn't kidding about shoes. I inched my way out over the slimy stones, feeling the water rising up my legs to my belly button. I wished I could see. Maybe there *was* something down there where the water got deep, something with beady eyes and razor teeth and long sucking tentacles waiting for a foot or a leg to come by, a lake squid waiting … for me … for dinner … *What was I doing out here?* My toes curled in so far they almost scratched my heels.

I held my breath and took another step forward. A rock gave way under my foot and I skidded forward. The water jumped up over my stomach. I felt as if Russell's fingers were prickling down my spine. Maybe, I thought, if I just leaned myself back, sort of, and sank down, I wouldn't have to go out farther. I moved my foot over to keep my balance, feeling carefully with my toes, and suddenly they sank in something soft.

"BWAH!" I screeched and jumped straight into

the air. Except you can't jump too high with a diving helmet on your head. The handle of the bucket banged on my chin, I tipped over and then the whole thing was filling with water and sinking. I grabbed for the bucket and kicked with my feet and screamed to keep the lake squid off and then my knees banged the bottom, the bucket came off, and I was pulling myself towards the shore on my hands, still yelling like crazy. I thought I was going to die for sure until I saw the water was only about six inches deep. I turned and looked behind me for the monster. All that was left was a big hunk of slimy green seaweed wrapped around one foot.

I thought Maggie and Russell were going to die, too, from laughing. Until my dad showed up. Then I thought we were just going to die, we were in trouble so fast.

Back at the cottage did Maggie and I ever get it. Crazy, stupid, dangerous, Rule Number One, didn't I just finish telling you, what did you think you were up to – we heard it all from my mom and dad. When they were done, my dad said we had to scrub the barbecue grill and help with dinner. We weren't allowed back in the water till day after tomorrow. As my dad marched off to change, I saw that his back was as red as his face. That wasn't going to help.

We did our chores with the grownups around, so we couldn't talk much. They were all cheery with each other but they wouldn't smile at us yet, like we'd been bad little kids.

It wasn't fair. Okay, so maybe a diving helmet

wasn't the smartest idea in the world, but I didn't make it up and I only went in the lake up to my waist. Besides, we'd already been swimming, so we still had permission, sort of. Hot tomatoes, I could probably swim better than my dad. All he did was that silly float, but *he* didn't need permission every time he stuck his toe in the lake, no matter what Great Aunt Gertrude said.

After dinner we got stuck helping Great Aunt Gertrude with the dishes. She washed, we dried. She talked all the time she washed and we could still barely keep up with the drying. She told us about the plants she could see from the kitchen window. It was pretty boring but at least she didn't act mad at us until she finished washing and gave us the X-ray eye. Here we go again, I thought.

Great Aunt Gertrude whispered, "That was a stupid thing to do this afternoon. In case you didn't know, mothers and fathers don't like to lose kids. *That's* why they're so upset. I used to tell your mother, Cyril, a championship swimmer can drown in a teacup. Understand?"

I thought I did maybe, almost, so I nodded. Maggie did, too.

"Fine. Make a mistake once and you're learning; twice and you're a fool. And if I were you I'd apologize."

I looked at the floor. I didn't like that part.

"Now." Great Aunt Gertrude dried her hands. "Show me how this helmet was supposed to work."

My head boinged up like a yo-yo. Maggie looked

like she didn't even know her mouth was open.

"Come on, come on," Great Aunt Gertrude rasped. Maggie told about it and how the air would get trapped underneath the helmet.

"Hold your horses there, Maggie," Great Aunt Gertrude said. "Did you know it works the other way round, too?" She took a glass and half filled it with water. "Water inside, air pushing down on top, right? In fact, the air pushes down so hard this can be like a suction cup." I thought about giant lake squids and shuddered. Great Aunt Gertrude went on. "I could stick this right smack to that roof beam."

"No way," Maggie said.

"Is that so?" said Great Aunt Gertrude. "C'mon then, kiddo, put your money where your mouth is. I'll bet you. I win, you apologize for today. You win, I do all the dishes. In fact, I bet I can get Cyril's dad stuck, too."

Maggie got her human computer look. Her eyes flicked from the glass to Great Aunt Gertrude to the beam, tic, tic, tic. "Bet," she said.

"Atta girl," Great Aunt Gertrude rasped. "Cyril, run get your dad."

A minute later, when I came back with my mom and dad, Great Aunt Gertrude was standing on a kitchen chair, stretching up to hold the glass of water to the ceiling with one hand. "Archie," she croaked, "the very man I'm looking for. Gimme a hand with this, will you? Just grab the broom there and prop this glass up for a minute till it sticks. It's too long a reach for me."

My dad got the broom and pressed the glass to the ceiling with the end of the handle. Great Aunt Gertrude climbed down and put the chair away. "Thanks, Archie," she said. "It shouldn't take long. C'mon kids, we'll check back in a minute." She marched us out to the porch. "Well, that's that. When are you paying up?"

"Huh?"

"Aunt Gertrude," my mom interrupted, "you really shouldn't. The poor guy has a sunburn." She was holding back a smile.

"Aw, Archie's a sport," said Great Aunt Gertrude. "He won't mind. We'll just leave him another minute or two. Wait till he calls. See Jan, I've got a little bet with these two here and they won't admit they've lost."

"We haven't," I said.

"Oh, yes you have, buster," Great Aunt Gertrude laughed. It sounded as if she was gargling with sand. "You see, the glass is stuck to the ceiling with the broom handle, and your dad is stuck to the handle – "

"Because he can't reach the glass and you put the chair away," Maggie groaned.

"But that's a trick," I complained. Grownups weren't supposed to trick you. "That's no fair."

"You bet your life it's a trick." Great Aunt Gertrude was laughing again.

"I'll remember that," Maggie said thoughtfully.

"Hey," came a voice from the kitchen, "what's going on around here?"

"I think," said my mom, "we'd better remember Archie as well."

We went back to the kitchen.

As my mom climbed up for the glass, Great Aunt Gertrude told my dad that stuff about making a mistake once and you're learning. He smiled with one corner of his mouth for about one microsecond. Then he asked my mom to put some more sunburn lotion on his back. I got a swampy feeling down in my stomach. Making him madder, and with a sunburn, probably hadn't been such a smart idea. But Great Aunt Gertrude just nodded at us over her glasses. "All right," she said, "now get in there and apologize."

I screwed up my face to complain. "You know what the bet was, sonny boy. Now I'm collecting. So, git!" She flicked a finger at the doorway.

I looked at Maggie. She shrugged like it was hopeless, so we shuffled along like pirates were making us walk the plank.

My parents were in their room. My mom was rubbing lotion on my dad and he was making faces. His back would have glowed in the dark.

"What is it, Cyril?" he said in a don't-bother-me voice. One side of his face was twisted up like he was sucking a lemon.

I looked down and picked at my T-shirt and said really small, "Sorry about doing diving this afternoon. It was dumb."

"Yeah," said Maggie.

I looked up from under my eyebrows. My mom smiled but for a second my dad looked like he was going to give us another speech. Then he sighed. "Okay. Everybody learns," and he smiled too. When he got the lemon-sucking look again, I knew it was from the sunburn.

From outside the room came a ripping sound. Great Aunt Gertrude was sitting at the porch table shuffling cards, a bowl of toothpicks in front of her. "Step right up," she barked. "Who wants to play poker?" and she showed us how until bedtime.

That night I lay in the top bunk and got used to my new room. Billions of crickets were squeaking in the dark outside my window screen and you could hear the lake swishing onto the beach. Light from the living-room shone through my doorway onto the little pile of rocks I put on the dresser. From the porch came grown-up voices and the scratching that was Great Aunt Gertrude's chuckle.

I sighed a big contented sigh. My bed had a sag in the middle that I fitted into perfectly. Tomorrow was going to be a good day. No more dumb stuff like diving helmets, no sir. I had a plan. Really three little ones. They were all genius. First off, I was going to collect lots of rocks, really beautiful ones. When I had the best rock collection in the world, some people might want some of it enough to trade a few things for it, like favours or being boss or who knows what. Things would be different when I had something great. Maybe I wouldn't even want to trade. Well, I'd trade a few and let Maggie run errands for me or something, just to show how big-hearted I was.

Then there was the Mr. Flynn letter. There were lots of old magazines around the cottage, so it would be a cinch. I figured I'd better keep working so it would be ready if I needed it. I didn't want to get stuck in any more banana-brained junk like today.

I could hear Maggie rustling around in her room. There was a scratching noise and then a whisper through the boards. "Cyril! You awake?"

"Yeah."

"My plan went okay today, huh? We just keep it up. The little squirt will never know what hit him. You've got to be careful though."

"Huh?" I said.

"You almost blew it there with the diving helmet. I don't want him getting mad, Cyril."

"Oh, come *on*," I hissed. "He didn't pick on *you* all day. *You* didn't help even a little. And you didn't have to laugh at me, either. I could have drowned, you know."

"Oh Cyril, get out. You looked funny, I couldn't help it. Anyway, you're supposed to be helping with this plan. Remember who saved you from giving Mr. Flynn a bikini? Hmmmm?"

"I already paid you back for that!" I said louder. Maggie was making me mad. "Anyway, I've got a way better plan."

"Shhhh," she said, "they'll hear you. What plan?"

"It's beautiful," I whispered. It was the third thing I'd thought of and Maggie was going to owe me big for it. "We don't need to be nice to Russell," I murmured. I could almost taste the words, they felt so good. "All we have to do is pull that glass of water trick on him and he's trapped. We just tell him we'll leave him stuck there holding the broom till dooms-day unless he gives us the tree house back. And know what? We'll use a bucket instead of a glass!" I nodded to myself in the dark and grinned the biggest, mean-est grin in the world.

Maggie said, "No."

"What?" I sat straight up in bed.

"*Shhhhhhh!* I said no, Cyril. No way. It's too risky and my tree house is too important. My way is better and that's final."

"Take off!" I whisper-screeched at the ceiling. "I hate your way. All I do is get picked on and look stupid."

Maggie started to argue back and then I started to argue back and we were so busy arguing that neither of us heard the car pull up or the footsteps or the knock on the back door. Just all of a sudden my dad's voice was louder and then two new voices were talking and the back screen door banged and there was a lot more talking and feet thumping around in the kitchen. We stopped arguing to listen.

"You're kidding," my dad was saying. "We didn't know you were coming," and my mom was saying, "Come on in, come on in." Then this lady's voice said, "Oh no, really, we're sorry to barge in like

71

this. We thought this one was Hummakers' cottage."

A man's voice said, "We just wanted to pick up the key." It was a familiar voice. A very familiar voice.

"Hey," I said to Maggie, through the ceiling. I dropped over the edge of the bunk to the floor and ran to my doorway. Maggie was craning her neck out to see.

"Is it him?" she whispered.

I leaned out and looked around Great Aunt Gertrude's back into the kitchen. A man and a woman were standing just inside the screen door. They were both wearing army shorts and sandals. The woman was carrying a straw purse. The man was twirling a ring of car keys and talking to my mom. Then he saw me.

"Hi Cyril," he called.

It was Mr. Flynn.

Scary Tale

THE NEXT THREE DAYS SHOULD have been fantastically terrific, but they weren't. They were weird. Mr. Flynn and his wife had rented their cottage from Russell's mother, just like us. I guess that was why she gave Mr. Flynn a card, the same as she did to my dad, and I felt pretty dumb for not figuring it out.

Now they were two cottages away, canoeing and fishing and hiking and doing all the neat stuff. I should have been doing it with them, except I wasn't allowed. My mom made up another rule: Don't Bug Your Teacher. He's on Vacation, Too. I said Mr. Flynn wasn't my teacher any more. My mom said that didn't matter. It felt as if I were outside this fantastic store with my pocket full of birthday money and the door was locked.

They were only staying for a week, then going camping. So I had to work fast to let Mr. Flynn know about how I got the tent for him. Once he found out, I knew he'd start asking me to do stuff with them, and that wouldn't count as Bugging. We'd have so much fun he'd ask me camping for sure, which would be perfect all by itself, and it would really bug Russell. Maggie, too.

Right now Maggie was no fun, either. She was still ga-ga about her Russell plan. I mean, at night she was whispering like crazy through the boards what a toad Russell was and how she wanted to shove beach balls up his nose. But in the daytime she and Russell were always doing stuff that I was no good at, or things you couldn't do with three. Maggie said she was hating it, but it sure didn't look like it. It gave me this jiggled-up feeling inside so I just quit hanging around with them and tried to make my own plan. Without Maggie it wasn't as much fun though, even if I didn't get bossed around.

What I did mostly was hang around on the beach, looking for rocks and trying to bump into Mr. Flynn. I was going to do the mystery letter really fast and sneak it over to their porch, but then I thought that if Mr. Flynn got the letter that way he'd guess it was from me. It wouldn't be like getting it in the mail. And if he guessed the letter was from me it would be like I was a sucky baby who wanted a pat on the head.

The beach was a pretty good idea, anyway. I mean, if Mr. Flynn saw some poor lonely kid wandering along all by himself he'd paddle over in his canoe and take the kid for a ride, right? And then Mr. Flynn and this kid would get talking and laughing and having a great time. If that kid happened to be me, then for sure the news about the tent would just pop out all by itself. It was perfect.

Except for one thing. Mr. Flynn was so busy doing all that neat junk with his wife that he never even seemed to notice me, except once in a while he'd wave from way far off. If Mr. Flynn was taking me camping with a two-man tent I was going to have to do something about her.

Then, one day I was on the beach, looking for good rocks at the very edge of the water when I heard stones crunching behind me and this voice said, "Hi Cyril." The voice sounded glad to see me, but I didn't know whose voice it was. I turned around and there was Mr. Flynn's wife.

"Uh … hi," I said back. I felt like a hot washcloth was plastered over my face. I looked down, then up again, then down. Mr. Flynn's wife was wearing shorts and a tennis shirt and sunglasses with red frames. Her hair was dark and she had a nice smile that stretched her lips way out. She tilted up her sunglasses and smiled even bigger.

"I'm Joyce," she said, "Mike's wife." Mike? Mr. Flynn. Mike sounded weird. She stuck out her hand to shake. I didn't know what else to do so I shook it. Then she smiled gigantic. "We haven't met, but I feel like we have, because Mike's told me so much about you."

My ears just about fell off. Mr. Flynn talked about me! I was too surprised to ask if it was good stuff or bad stuff. I swallowed.

"Are you collecting stones, Cyril? Me, too." She held up a plastic bag. "Have you got any good ones?"

I pulled some out of my pockets. "I got these today," I said, or almost did. I couldn't seem to get my voice to work right. My tongue felt like a giant sponge.

"Wow, Cyril, these are *won*derful. Will you show me where you've been looking? Can I look there, too?"

I showed her in the shallow water and we started looking for rocks together. After a little bit my tongue started to feel okay again. Joyce said she always hunted for rocks at the beach. I said, "Me, too," even though I'd never been at a beach before. Then she asked what I was going to do with the rocks I found and I said I didn't know. Joyce said she was going to put all hers in this fancy bowl on top of an antique washing stand that she and Mike, I mean, Mr. Flynn, were fixing up. That sounded pretty boring but Joyce seemed to like it so I said, "The only thing about rocks is they don't look as shiny when they get dry."

"I know what you mean, Cyril. You know what I'm going to do? I'm going to fill the bowl with water so they'll always sparkle."

"Neat," I said, and it was.

We waded slowly along the shoreline peering in the water and grabbing up rocks and talking away at about five hundred miles an hour. It felt excellent to have the sun all hot on my shoulders and the cool water sloshing through my running shoes.

"So what have you and Maggie been up to all summer, Cyril?"

Before I knew it I was telling Joyce a whole bunch of stuff. By the time I went up for lunch she'd heard about Maggie's clubhouse plan and Great Aunt Gertrude and the diving helmet and the duel with the eggs and everything, except I left out a couple of the bits where dumb stuff happened to me and I made some other stuff better.

At lunch I told everyone all about collecting rocks with Joyce, but I left out that I'd blabbed about our whole summer.

"Now Cyril, please don't bother the Flynns too much," my mom said. "Remember our rule."

I started to moan and groan how it wasn't fair, but Great Aunt Gertrude interrupted. "Hold your horses, you two. Your dear old Auntie Gert has a suggestion."

I wasn't sure I liked the sound of that. Great Aunt Gertrude didn't scare me quite as much as she used to, but you never could tell. "There's no use pretending your Mr. Flynn is off in Timbuktu when he's right next door, but you don't want to bother him either. So instead of chasing after him, why don't we have a beach fire tomorrow night and invite everybody over? Then we can all have a visit and I'll meet this fella I keep hearing about."

"A beach fire?" My dad sounded confused.

"A campfire on the beach," my mom explained. "We'll roast some marshmallows and hot dogs, have a night swim if it's warm enough. Auntie Gert, it sounds terrific. And if the Flynns agree to come," she looked at me, "we don't bother them until then.

Right?" I nodded. "Settled," said my mom. "Maybe Auntie Gert will tell some stories, too."

"You bet your life I will, dearie. And we'll have a sing-song."

"Hey," I cried. "Mr. Flynn plays the guitar!" This was turning out so great I could hardly believe it. Even Maggie looked interested. Great Aunt Gertrude couldn't even guess how excellent it really was.

"Well Cyril," she said to me, "after lunch you and I and Maggie will walk over and find out if Mr. Flynn brought that guitar along. And then you two can invite the Hummakers as well."

"Okay!" we both said. My okay was for inviting Mr. Flynn and Joyce. Maggie's was for inviting Russell. I don't know how I knew it, but I did.

That afternoon we asked everybody to come and they said yes. The next morning my dad and Great Aunt Gertrude and I drove into town. Maggie was busy with Russell. My dad went to the grocery store. Great Aunt Gertrude and I went to the hardware store. After I'd told her how Joyce was going to put rocks in a bowl of water, Aunt Gertrude had said she had a better way – paint the rocks with shellac. Then, she said, they'd be shiny even when they were dry. Now she bought me a little tin of shellac and a paint brush. When I thanked her she said, "That's all right, kiddo. Just do a nice one for me."

"Sure."

Then, right there on the street, she started to sing. " 'Rocks in your so-ocks and slugs on your toes, There's a skunk in the outhouse so ho-old your nose.' We used to sing that at the cottage when your mother was a girl. I wish I could remember the rest of it."

Was she kidding me or what, I wondered. Then I gave up. It was too hot to worry.

Going along the sidewalk felt like walking on a barbecue. By the time we met my dad I was turning into a puddle. Aunt Gertrude was panting. Her face was all red and you could see drops of sweat. Was I ever glad when we got out of town and felt the cool lake breeze coming through the car windows.

I sat in the back seat and thought about how great the beach fire was going to be. Mr. Flynn and Joyce were coming, which made up for Russell and his parents. I could hear the singing, see the fire blazing and feel the coolness of the dark water. I wondered what kind of stories Great Aunt Gertrude would tell.

In fact the only thing in the whole world better than the beach fire might be this afternoon, collecting firewood, because Mr. Flynn was going to come. Maybe he and I would have to rescue all the others from a bear or a mountain lion. Or I'd help him lift a log that no one else could move. Then we'd do some canoeing and it would come out about the tent and …. By the time the car got back to the cottage I was half way through our next adventure, where he and Joyce and I were diving for sunken treasure and fighting pirates. I'd decided that we'd get a bigger tent so she could come too.

At lunch time Maggie said that she and Russell

had found tons of wood up by the creek, and Mr. Hummaker had said we could take the row-boat over and load it up.

After lunch Maggie and Russell and I were with my dad, clearing a flat space for everyone to sit on the beach, when Mr. Flynn came up.

He didn't look like a teacher at all. He was wearing his army shorts and a straw hat with the edge bent down all around. His moustache twirled up so far it almost met the hat.

My dad told him we were going to use the boat, which was over by Russell's. Mr. Hummaker was snoozing in a lounge chair right next to it. "All right!" said Mr. Flynn, just like a kid. "How about I get the canoe and, if I can get another paddler, we can do two loads at once."

I bounced around in the sand a little to keep from screaming, "MEEEEEEEE," right in his face.

Russell sniffed and said, "I'd better stay with my boat." Maggie said, "I guess I'll go with Russell." For a microsecond I thought *"Traitor,"* but Mr. Flynn was saying, "How about it, Cyril?" and then I didn't care what Maggie wanted. I nodded as if yeah, I guess I can help you this once. That saved me from talking. I couldn't have got my mouth open without a crow-bar.

"Great," Mr. Flynn said. "Let's get at it."

I followed him back to the other cottage. We rolled over his canoe and he laid two paddles and a hatchet in the bottom. Then we put on our lifejackets and I helped carry the canoe down to the water.

"Okay Cyril, you're in the bow." Mr. Flynn held the canoe steady while I climbed in and sort of tiptoed along the very centre part to the front. The canoe felt very, very tippy. I held tight to the sides with both hands all the way, boy. Mr. Flynn pushed us out into deeper water. I felt him climb in the other end, and when the canoe wobbled I practically squeezed my fingers through the sides. Then came bumping and thumping and suddenly the end of a paddle slid under my nose. "Take this, Cyril. Canoeing is a two-man job." Mr. Flynn showed me how to use the paddle and we were gliding off across the water.

"Good work, Cyril," he called. "Keep it up. Hey, have you ever canoed before?"

"No." The paddle felt like a telephone pole.

"No kidding?" Mr. Flynn sounded like he didn't believe me. Hey, I thought, I was doing okay. Maybe the paddle wasn't *that* heavy after all. I tried a little harder.

"Nice and steady now," came Mr. Flynn's voice. I looked back at the row-boat pulling away from shore. It went kind of zig-zaggy. My dad was having trouble rowing straight. I shook my head a little and smiled. Maybe Mr. Flynn or I could give him a couple of pointers later on.

The sunlight flashed everywhere off the ripply water. Out on the lake there was no sound except the glip of our paddles in the water and the slapping of the tiny waves against the canoe. Everything was so absolutely exactly excellently perfect that I didn't even want to breathe. I was this incredibly famous super-brave explorer setting off up a mysterious, uncharted river.

"I hear you've been having a busy summer, Cyril." The words made me jump. I thought back to rock collecting with Joyce. What exactly *had* I said? I couldn't remember, but I would have bet you a million dollars it was something stupid. My stomach dropped to the bottom of the lake.

"Maggie's still at war with Russell, huh?" Mr. Flynn chuckled. "Boy, those two never give up, do they?"

"Uh, yeah," I said. "No."

"And you went diving?"

"Not exactly." I didn't look back at him. My face felt like I got instant sunburn. How could I have told Joyce all that stuff? It all sounded so dumb, so little-kiddy.

"And wasn't there an egg fight?" asked Mr. Flynn.

Every question made me shrink an inch. We weren't supposed to talk about dumb Cyril stuff. I'd thought adventure talk would just happen, but out here paddling along my brain had been washed overboard. How come I hadn't solved a murder or been a spy or built a robot? There had to be something neat I could say.

As we passed the creek I thought of the perfect

thing. "You know that creek?" I said. "It's bottomless and it's haunted by somebody who drowned there." Now that was adventure talk. Now we'd work around to the tent, I knew it.

"Well, I don't know about haunted," Mr. Flynn said, "but it's not bottomless. I dropped a fishing line in the other day and I got slack awfully fast. I make it about four feet deep in the middle. It's the muddy bottom that fools you."

"Oh." I had shrunk to Grade One size and soon I was going to be back to crawling.

"Who told you all that anyway?" Mr. Flynn asked.

"Russell," I muttered.

"Of course," Mr. Flynn said, and then we were pulling in to shore.

We carried the canoe up onto the beach and started to gather pieces of driftwood. Then the rowboat pulled in and the others started to help. I worked extra hard to make up for being dumb in the canoe, but even that backfired. Mr. Flynn said I didn't need to drag over such big pieces when there was lots of small stuff around that we wouldn't need to chop up.

I shrank right down to diaper size.

"Told you," said Russell, "little stuff is better," as he went by with an armload of wood for the rowboat. He had not told me, but he was gone before I could get him for it – or for telling lies about the creek.

When both the boats were loaded up, we climbed

back in the canoe and pushed off while the others fooled with the row-boat. I looked back over my shoulder, called "Get back before supper, you guys," and took a huge stroke with my paddle to zoom us out into the lake. It was perfect, except my paddle missed the water. I rolled right into the lake and tipped the whole canoe.

Everyone but me was laughing by the time we got things fixed up. Mr. Flynn even told me he'd tipped canoes, lots of times, but I didn't believe it. Everything was wrecked. I'd been just like my dad in a canoe and now Mr. Flynn wouldn't take me with him again, let alone invite me mountain climbing. I said stupid things, I picked stupid wood, and then I tipped the stupid boat and soaked the stupid wood. I should have just stayed home and looked for stupid rocks.

It wasn't any better when we got back to the cottage. After we built the fire and stacked the wood, my dad and Mr. Flynn went to get a beer. Russell turned into a complete motormouth and told me I should get a job as a tightrope walker because I was so good at balancing.

"Oh yeah?" I snarled back. "What do you know? That creek is not bottomless, so why don't you be a professional liar? Mr. Flynn says it's four feet deep."

"How's he know?" said Russell. "He jump in head first?"

Before I could yell back, Russell's mom called him. I waited till he was running off and then made about fourteen disgusting faces at his back. It didn't help much.

"How come he had to be here, anyway?" I roared to Maggie, kicking hard at the sand. "He's a jerkface. Everything's wrong because of him." That wasn't really true, but I was tired of stuff being my fault.

"He's a jerkface, all right," Maggie said, like it didn't matter. She just kept fussing with the driftwood. "But he is pretty smart, Cyril. Not as smart as me, but pretty smart. You should see the fort we started. We made this lookout post out of – "

I couldn't believe my ears. A fort? With the Toad-Faced Tree House Thief?

"You're making a *fort* with that dwork?" I yelled.

"Oh Cyril, it's all part of the plan," said Maggie. "Tease him back if he bugs you. Who cares if he's smarter than you?"

"Just because he's smart doesn't make him nice," I hissed back. "I thought you hated him." I started for our cottage.

"I do hate him," Maggie called, but you could tell by her voice that she didn't, not any more.

"Cyril, we're *supposed* to play with him, remember? Anyway, he's going to camp day after tomorrow!"

I kept moving. Even one more day was too much of Russell.

"You play with him," I called over my shoulder, "if you *like* him so much. Does he make you feel all lovey-dovey?"

"Just 'cause *you* follow Mr. Flynn around like a puppy dog!" Maggie shouted.

That did it. I stomped up the stairs like I was going to smash them into toothpicks. Probably Maggie and Russell would spend the whole beach fire teasing me about how much I liked the water and how you couldn't keep me out of it, ha ha ha. Everybody'd treat me like the little kid. Well, if they thought I was that dumb I wouldn't go to their stupid beach fire. Not if they paid me. They could all go laugh at someone else.

I waited till dessert time and then I said I didn't feel like going to the beach fire. The grownups started talking all at once. What about the stories, and the swim, and the food? No, I said. I was going to stay in the cottage and shellac my rock collection.

My mom felt my forehead about ten times and asked was I feeling all right, but at last they gathered up their sweaters and flashlight and pop and hot dogs and marshmallows and chairs and started across the lawn for the beach.

"You're sure you'll be okay?" called my mom. "You'll let us know if you need anything?" I nodded my head. "Well, have fun," she said.

I stood on the porch and watched them go. My dad was leading the way, then Aunt Gertrude, talking as usual, her earlobes flapping away, then my mom, then Maggie. They looked like explorers heading off for six months in the jungle they had so much stuff. At the top of the stairs Maggie looked back at the cottage. I almost yelled to wait, but then she shrugged and headed down to the beach.

At first being alone was almost fun. It was still pretty light out and I sat at the table with my shellac and brush and the rocks all spread out on newspapers so I could paint the top half of each and then set it out to dry. Later I'd turn them over and do the bottom. The breeze had died down and the lake was quiet so you could hear everybody gather around and get comfortable and ask where I was. I knew someone like Mr. Flynn or Joyce would come up and ask me to come on down. I'd hem and haw and then do it as a favour. Or maybe, they'd have such a good time with me they wouldn't want to go back. I twisted the top off the shellac and got to work so I'd look busy.

Instead it just got darker. Millions of crickets began to chirp. You could see the glow of the fire above the edge of the bank and hear crackling mixed with the voices. Wispy bits of smoke rose in the air.

I brushed shellac on a few rocks and set them down to dry. It was messy and the shellac stank so much I had to stop after a bit. I never knew I'd gathered up so many rocks.

From the beach came a strum on Mr. Flynn's guitar and then they were all singing "Michael, Row the Boat Ashore." I leaned my head against the door screen and listened. Nobody was missing me down there. Probably they liked it better without me. Maybe I could run away and get a job on a farm, I thought. Then my dad's head popped up in the grey light at the top of the steps. I dove back for the table.

"Everything okay, Cyril?"

"Ye-ah, I'm painting the rocks."

"Okay, well come on down if you want to."

When his head disappeared again, I went back to the screen door and slipped outside. It wouldn't hurt to peek at what was going on.

They were singing about down by the riverside as I snuck across the lawn to the edge of the bank. I flopped down and spied through the tall weeds. Everyone was in a big circle around the fire, singing and swaying to the music, their faces all shiny in the light. My mom and dad were clapping their hands and Great Aunt Gertrude was bouncing her foot in the sand. Over beside Mr. Flynn, Maggie and Russell were watching everybody and pretending to sing the way you do with the anthem in school. At the end of the song my dad sang this high note and everybody clapped and laughed and called for another song. Russell leaned over and whispered something to Maggie. She giggled. I wanted to drop a piano on him.

Back inside the cottage I turned on the light by the table and plopped down in my chair. I listened to more songs, sliding down until I could barely see over the table top. From there the rocks on the table looked like boulders on an alien planet. I wished *I* was on an alien planet.

The night was black dark now and all you could see outside was a tiny patch of light from the fire. Sparks wavered up into the sky like fireflies and blinked out. Something rustled in the grass. I turned my head to listen. It was gone. I glanced behind me into the dim cottage. It looked a little spooky. I'd never been in it all by myself before. Could the ghost come all the way from the creek? I shuddered and pretended it was a shiver.

Now voices were asking Great Aunt Gertrude for a story. She started this one about how an Indian brave stole fire for people. It was pretty good too, except that right in the middle of it came this *bump, bump, bump, bump* on the porch screen. I shot up in my chair. *Bump, bump, bump.* There it was again! Then I saw it was a big moth trying to get through the screen to the lamplight. I started to breathe again. Maybe, I thought, I'd shellac some more rocks, just to keep busy. Besides, they'd be right there if I needed to throw them.

Great Aunt Gertrude started another story about a guy who kept tricking the devil. It made everyone laugh, except me. I didn't like the way she kept making the devil pop up beside the guy, snap, just like that.

The cottage was making all these funny creaking noises and I kept whipping around to check, in case someone came out of a puff of smoke. Then everyone laughed all of a sudden and *that* made me jump and I knocked over the tin of shellac. Nail polish smell filled the cottage. I hopped around trying to wipe everything up with the newspapers, and by the time I was done I was dizzy and sticky all over.

The cottage was getting spookier. The shadows in the bedroom doorways seemed to move. I pushed my chair right back against the inside wall so nothing could get me from behind.

Down on the beach it got very quiet. The fire popped. Great Aunt Gertrude's voice got mysterious: "Now this story is a little bit different. It's supposed to have happened around here, you see. Years and years ago I heard it, back when I first camped up this way and I'll tell you, it made me wonder. Of course, he'd be long dead now so it doesn't matter the way it did then. That is, if the story's true at all."

Who would be dead? I opened my ears for every word and I didn't want to hear any of them.

"Now it seems there was a lonely farmhouse just to the north of here, the Baldwin place, I think it was called, and Mr. Baldwin was, let's say, a bit cracked. He was a giant of a man, strong as an ox. They say he used to be a lumberjack, because he was always carrying a huge, two-bladed axe. He even carried it in the house, stood it up in a corner while he ate or slept. It was so sharp, folks said, he shaved with it. Still, no one would have thought of … murder … at least not until that one night …. " Great Aunt Gertrude's voice growled away.

Something scraped at the back door of the cottage. I sat up: nothing.

"It was the middle of summer," Great Aunt Gertrude's voice croaked on. "Uneasy weather. Hot, overcast. Thunder rumbled all day long but it never rained. That afternoon a neighbour saw Mr. Baldwin out in the barnyard sharpening the axe at a grindstone. Sparks flying, his big leg pumping the pedal. Every so often, he'd stop and test the blade on a hair he'd pluck from his head, then sharpen some more. His arm muscles were bulging, and his eyes staring as the grindstone shrieked like a mad thing and the thunder rolled across the sky .... "

A prickling feeling crept across my head, exactly as if someone were gently parting the hairs on top. With an axe. I held tight to the chair so it wouldn't run away without me and forced myself to look up: nothing. The whole night had gone still. What happened to the crickets?

I heard Great Aunt Gertrude saying, "That night, for miles around, everyone heard screams from the Baldwin place. And when they got there they found .... "

Suddenly I wanted to be down at that beach fire. I leaped to the door. And stopped. What might be out there, waiting? Besides, everyone would guess I was scared. Then I saw the watermelon.

It was on the couch where the sweaters had been piled up; it should have been taken down to the beach. I could take it to them right now, as a favour, and then just decide to stick around. Besides, if a maniac charged me I could bowl it at his legs and trip him, or if he was close and swung his axe at me maybe he'd hit the melon instead.

I grabbed the watermelon, stuffed my toes into my beach runners and softly pushed the door open, so the maniac wouldn't hear me. I slipped outside and caught the door with my foot so it wouldn't slam. All I could see were shadows, like haunted houses.

Great Aunt Gertrude's voice was whispering now.

"Then someone noticed strange tracks leading across the farmyard in the moonlight. They were heading towards the woods. Half the track was the print of a man's boot, but the other part was a long wet smear in the dirt where the other foot should be. Blood. He must have chopped his foot too, so he walked like this." From the beach I heard thump, *scraape*, thump, *scraaape*.

I hurried across the lawn, weaving from side to side so I'd be harder to hit with an axe. My shoes were shuffling and flapping because I hadn't put them on right. One slipped, I tripped and landed on the watermelon.

"Bwoof!" I gasped. My shoe flew into the bushes.

"What was that?" I heard my mom's voice. Should I yell out that it was me? Then I had a terrible thought: *what if it wasn't me they heard?* My whole body turned to water. I scrunched up under the trees holding my breath and closing my eyes to make me invisible.

"It's that darn racoon," I heard Mr. Hummaker say. Chairs scraped on the stones and it got quiet again.

"Well," Great Aunt Gertrude went on, "they followed those tracks into the woods as far as they could. And all through the night, just ahead of them they thought they could hear the thump, *scrape*, thump, *scraape* of his feet. At dawn they got to the edge of the swamp, about three miles from here, and the tracks stopped. Now some say he drowned in that swamp, but others say .... "

Three miles from here! My gulp was so hard my stomach almost came out my ears. I moaned a little.

"What was that?" snapped a voice – Russell's.

I had to get out of there. I crawled fast, dragging along the watermelon. If I stood up I knew *his* hand would grab me. I dragged the watermelon across the top step to the beach and bumped it down to the next. At the fire someone screamed and it got quiet. I dragged the melon and bumped it down again, but it was too slow. He'd get me for sure. I stood up to run. Something brushed across the back of my neck. I opened my mouth to scream but nothing came out. Then my foot slipped and the watermelon was bouncing and I was falling down into the sand and then I was up and running, screaming "SAVE MEEEEEEE!" The axe maniac was right behind me and the sand was slowing me down.

Maggie was screaming. Somebody roared a swear word and everyone was yelling. Russell was hiding behind Maggie and pointing at Great Aunt Gertrude. "Take the old lady, take the old lady! Leave me alone!"

Then WHAM! Great big hands grabbed me and all my bones rattled. I swung and kicked and yelled.

It was my dad.

"Cyril! It's Cyril!" the voices went up. Suddenly everyone was squeaking and groaning with relief. I couldn't believe it. My mom and Joyce had hands up at their necks, panting. Russell's parents had their mouths open, Mr. Flynn was shaking his head and Maggie was looking from Russell to me. That was when I figured out it was me all the yelling was about, not some monster behind me. Great Aunt Gertrude was sighing a huge sigh and looking hard at me over her glasses. Something told me I'd wrecked her story.

"Cyril, what are – look at you!" My mom was staring as if I was from another planet. I looked at me. I was covered with sand everywhere I'd been sticky with shellac. Even on my face and in my hair.

I said, "I, I was ...." but I didn't know what I was. Great Aunt Gertrude was still looking at me, hard. I just knew I was going to get it.

"Wait a minute," my dad said suspiciously, and then started to grin. "Gertrude!" He swung around to stare at her. Then all the grownups were gasping and laughing and saying "Oh no," and "You *didn't*," and I was thinking, *huh?*

My dad said, "C'mon now, Gertrude, this has your prints all over it. Did you and young Frankenstein here cook this up as a little surprise ending? What about it, huh?"

I started to say "Whaaaaaat?" but Great Aunt Gertrude shook her head and crooked her finger at me. I went over to her, slowly. She stood me by her chair, looked me up and down, brushed off some sand, and put one arm around my shoulder. Then she raised one eyebrow and said, "That's for us to know and you to find out. Maybe we did and maybe we didn't, but you know, great minds think alike. Right Cyril?"

"R-right," I said, and tried to close my mouth. Great Aunt Gertrude smiled a secret smile. "We *will* say it's a made-up story and that it's time to roast some marshmallows." And when they all stopped laughing, that's what we did.

Mr. Flynn got his guitar and my mom and Aunt Gertrude taught him their cottage song.

"Rocks in your so-ocks and slugs on your toes,
The skunk's in the outhouse so ho-old your nose,
To swat the mosquitoes you need a shotgun,
Oh, life at the cottage is plenty of fun!"

The rest of the song was a whole bunch more about the horrible stuff that happened at cottages. It sounded scary but it was fun. It was a Great Aunt Gertrude kind of song, I guess. Anyway, I liked it.

Maggie and Russell and I roasted marshmallows for everyone kneeling right by the fire. Russell was in the middle.

"Nice try, Cyril," he said, "but I knew it was you all along. Not like *some* people." And he looked around like he was brain of the universe.

"Yeah, right," said Maggie.

Russell was really, truly surprised. "What's the matter with you?" he asked.

Maggie looked at him for a long moment. Then she stood up, walked over to my other side and plopped down again. "Russell," she said slowly, "you don't need to eat marshmallows, you are one." She pulled her marshmallow stick out of the fire and blew out the flame. "Want one, Cyril?" I could barely believe it. I took the really gooey burned one off the end and popped it in my mouth. Maggie took the next one.

"That was a really good trick, Cyril," she said. "You two sure kept it a secret." She leaned closer and whispered, "It was so good it almost scared *me.*"

I was about to yell "Almost!" when Great Aunt Gertrude raised one eyebrow. I decided not to say anything. Lately it seemed I was a lot smarter when I shut up. Besides, I was already smiling *and* chewing, and you weren't supposed to talk with a mouth full.

Socks Full of Rocks

"**C**YRIL," MAGGIE SAID, "I HAVE GOT A stupendously super-incredible plan for you."

It was the day after Russell left for camp and we were sitting at the picnic table in front of our cottage. We were supposed to be sorting through my rock collection. The rocks, all shellacked and shiny, were spread out over the table top. You couldn't really see the newspaper bits stuck to some of them. I didn't want to get rid of any of them but my dad said that I had to or we'd have to hire a truck to haul them home. I could see us barrelling down the highway in a huge truck full of rocks, but my dad gave me his you're-acting-stupid smile, so now I had to choose.

Maggie was no help. She spent the whole time swatting flies and grumbling about how hot it was. She couldn't have cared less about rocks. The only thing she liked in my whole collection was a lump of glass.

It was green and worn and scratched and frosted all over by the sand and water. Great Aunt Gertrude called it beach glass. She said it was part of one of those knobbly things on electrical poles. Whatever it was, it was big as my fist and there was a tunnel up inside it where it looked as if you could screw something in. The glass was clear there and if you held it up to the sun and squinted it looked like a galaxy exploding inside.

I told Maggie she could have it if I got to pick everything we did for the whole rest of the summer. Maggie told me to forget it, like I knew she would. Still, I got nervous when she started talking about plans. You never could tell what I might end up owing her.

"You're really going to love this plan for sure, Cyril."

"Uhhhhhh-huh," I said cautiously. Keeping my mouth shut was my new rule, since the beach fire.

"Don't you want to know what it is?"

"Uh-uh. I'm busy." I nodded at the rocks.

"Yeah, right," snorted Maggie, and looked at her watch. "We've been out here for twenty-seven minutes, Cyril, and you haven't gotten rid of one rock."

"I have too," I said in a no-fair voice, and I pointed to four little ones.

"You said *maybe* you'd get rid of those."

"Well, maybe I will."

Maggie rolled her eyes. I was glad we were partners again but now it was as if I'd always known it would work out that way. After all, Russell was a jerkface and I wasn't. Russell had stayed jerky. After he'd gone, we found he'd scoffed all the good beach junk he and Maggie had collected. Maggie was even more disgusted with him than before. I just listened to her complain and didn't say "I told you" more than ten times, maybe.

So everything was the way it was supposed to be. I knew now I hadn't been *that* scared the night of the beach fire, not as scared as everyone on the beach, anyway. They were totally petrified; I was just being careful.

Besides, Maggie wasn't the only person in the world who thought I was okay. Everybody had told me what a great trick surprising everybody had been and after a bit I got thinking maybe I *had* planned it. Well, not planned it exactly, but that all along I'd kind of guessed what would happen, sort of, in a geniusy kind of way.

So, everything was pretty good, except that we still weren't allowed to hang around with Mr. Flynn and Joyce and they still didn't know about the tent. And I had to get rid of some rocks.

I picked up a couple of sparkly red and white ones; I had a bunch like that. These looked pretty good though, so I put them back and shuffled some others around. Maggie sighed and bounced her knees up and down. "Look Cyril, you're being a bozo not listening, but I'm going to do you a big favour and tell you this plan anyway. You have to get rid of some rocks, right? And Mr. Flynn never found out about you and his tent, right? And you want to hang around with them a little, right?"

I stopped shuffling rocks and looked at her. That didn't count as talking. Maggie smiled her I'm-a-genius smile. "I can solve all three things at once. Just for you, Cyril, from the Maple Avenue Marvel."

I couldn't help myself. "How?" I breathed.

"You'll have to do three things back for me," Maggie warned, but I was already imagining scuba diving in Antarctica with Mr. Flynn and Joyce.

"Sure," I stuttered, "sure, sure, sure." I knew when to keep my mouth shut and when to talk.

"Promise?" said Maggie. "Cross your heart and hope to die, double stamp it?"

"Yeahyeahyeahyeahyeah," I said. "Come on."

Maggie said, "Okay, here's what you do: pick a bunch of those rocks and give them to Joyce. Then, when they thank you, you say, 'It was nothing. Rocks are a lot easier to get than that tent was,' and you laugh a little bit. Then you slap your hand over your mouth and look embarrassed. They'll start asking what you mean, and you pretend like you don't want to tell, but you let them find out, by accident like, how it happened."

"I can't tell about the bikini," I gasped.

"Of course not, Cyril. That would make you look stupid. You talk about how hard it was to get the money and pick the tent."

"I get it," I said. "Like we had to walk to the store in a blizzard or something."

"Or something," Maggie said. "They'll probably invite you camping if you do it right."

"Think so? Oh wow, thanks Maggie!" I shouted.

"And then you'll have to do three things for me."

"No sweat," I laughed. "Any time you think of something."

"Oh, I've already thought of them," Maggie said.

"You have?" The giggles drained out of me like water from a bathtub.

"Naturally I've thought of them," said Maggie, "that's what being a Marvel is all about. Now here they are, Cyril, three little things." She ticked them off on her fingers. "Number One: While you're talking with Mr. Flynn and Joyce, you tell them what a great kid I am and how we need a clubhouse. Maybe they'll let us borrow their tent when they're not camping."

I said uneasily, "I dunno if I – "

"Don't worry," Maggie interrupted, "I'll tell you what to say. Now, Number Two: I get to use the air mattress whenever I want."

"Ohhhhhhhhh." My dad had just bought the air mattress and Maggie and I were already arguing about whose turn it was and how long we each got it for. Maggie frowned at me as if I was a dumb little kid. I sighed and nodded okay.

"Good," said Maggie. "Number Three: I get the beach glass."

"What? No way!" I pounced for the picnic table even though Maggie hadn't moved.

"Cyril. I made up this plan just for you and practically all I want is a dumb old piece of glass. You get the whole rest of those rocks almost."

"Yeahbut – "

Maggie glared and put her hands on her hips. "And you promised double stamped it," she said like a machine gun.

I was stuck. I said slowly, "But only if it all works."

"It'll work," said Maggie, and she reached for the glass. I grabbed it up. "After," I said.

Maggie smiled again, but now she looked like an evil mastermind. "Okay, after. But be careful with my glass, Cyril. Anyway, I'm boiling. So go ask Great Aunt Gertrude to come swimming with us. I want to use the air mattress."

That started me yelling all over again. It wasn't the swimming or the air mattress part, I was boiling too. The tough part was asking Great Aunt Gertrude and she was the only grownup around to ask. My mom had driven into town to do some shopping and my dad was down at Hummakers' place calling in to the newspaper. I wasn't usually scared to ask Great Aunt Gertrude stuff any more but this morning she'd told us not to bug her, she was too busy.

Great Aunt Gertrude was whipping around doing stuff extra hard. She'd already walked to the farm up the road with my mom and picked a whole bunch of strawberries and now she was baking a pie. I knew it wasn't a good time to ask but Maggie said I'd promised and she wanted to use the air mattress right now. I made my first-bite-of-broccoli face and headed for the cottage.

Inside it was even hotter, like sitting in the beach fire. Great Aunt Gertrude was at the sink in the kitchen washing up some baking things. A fresh-baked pie sat on the stove behind her and on the counter was a bowl full of strawberries. Great Aunt Gertrude's face was so red that she looked like a strawberry herself. Even her fluffy yellow hair was drooping. I felt the sweat starting to prickle all over me.

"Hi Auntie Gert." I called her what my mom did. I was going to take my time about asking, until I found out if she was in a good mood.

"Cyril," she crowed, "have a berry." She shook water off her hands and popped one in my mouth. "It's not chips but you'll like it. You'd better, kiddo. You're going to be eating plenty of them."

I chewed and swallowed. It didn't taste that bad. "Aren't you having one?" I asked. She sounded pretty happy.

Aunt Gertrude leaned closer and whispered, "Between you and me and the wall, Cyril, I stuffed myself while I was picking them."

She had to be in a good mood for sure, so I whispered back, "Isn't that illegal?" like I was all scared.

She straightened up and gave me the evil eye over her dark glasses. "Hey buster, are you accusing me of something?"

In one second flat I turned into Cyril the Jelly Boy. "No," I stammered. "N-no!"

"I should hope not," she said, and turned back to the sink.

I started to breathe again. She was teasing. Wasn't

she? That was the thing with Great Aunt Gertrude: you never could tell.

"Just don't tell on me, Cyril, that's all I ask." Then she winked. "I bet you can't tell me the difference between illegal and unlawful."

I couldn't and I didn't care; I just wanted to ask about swimming. But Great Aunt Gertrude loved getting you with questions like that. She was as bad as Maggie. I made a couple of dumb guesses because I was supposed to. Then she said, "Give up? Unlawful is against the law, but ill eagle is a sick bird."

She started chuckling like mad at her own joke.

"Auntie Gert, will you come swimming with us? We're boiling."

Aunt Gertrude paused and puffed a big breath up at the damp hairs on her forehead. "Cyril," she said, "you're on. I'm nearly cooked myself. This heat is making me dizzy." She turned off the water and stood leaning on the counter for a second. Then, "I'll get my suit on. And I'll meet you outside."

Maggie and I already had our swim-suits on, so we grabbed the air mattress and waited under the trees by the beach steps. After a few minutes Great Aunt Gertrude didn't come so Maggie went back to the cottage. She came out looking mixed up. You didn't see Maggie looking that way very often.

"What's going on?" I asked.

"She said she's coming," Maggie said. Then, in a whisper, "She's got her bathing-suit on but she's wearing a *sweater* over it. She said she felt shivery all of a sudden. Can you believe it?" Maggie fanned herself with her hand. "Your Aunt Gertrude is weird, Cyril."

We waited a few more minutes until even in the shade, we were feeling like baked potatoes about to explode. Back we went to the cottage and called to Aunt Gertrude. There was no answer. We climbed the steps to the screen door and looked inside. Everything stopped. Sitting in a chair with her *sweater* over her swim-suit was Great Aunt Gertrude. All slumped over.

"Aunt Gertrude?" I called. "Aunt Gertrude?" She didn't move. Something went fluttery inside of me. Maggie was staring at me with huge eyes.

Then I was yelling for my dad.

"He can't hear you," Maggie said, very fast. "We'll have to get him. C'mon." She started down the steps.

I said, "You go, you're fastest. I better stay here." I didn't know what I was going to do but I didn't want to leave Aunt Gertrude.

"Right," Maggie called. She was gone before I could yell for her to wait up.

Great Aunt Gertrude looked so terrible I wanted to hide in the bushes till my dad came. But I couldn't do that. Softly I pulled the door open and tiptoed inside.

Aunt Gertrude's face was all red. Her glasses had slipped and her jaw was hanging to one side. She was breathing in shuddery little gasps. I swallowed hard. What did doctors do? I tried to remember stuff but my brains were all shaky. All I knew for sure was that they took your pulse and put wet cloths on your forehead.

I made myself reach out and lift her wrist. It was heavy and hot and soft. I felt around for the pulse the way we learned in health class. It was running like a racing car engine. I was so surprised I dropped her arm. Was her pulse good or bad? I didn't know so I ran to the washroom and soaked a face cloth in cold water. In the movies people always yelled for hot water, but Great Aunt Gertrude felt like a furnace already.

I raced back with the cloth and held it on her forehead with one hand. Her face looked grey now underneath the red and her breath wheezed. With my other hand I grabbed a magazine off the table and started fanning her like crazy to try and wake her up. It didn't work. The only thing that moved was a vein that flickered in the side of her head. "Come on," I said through my teeth. *"Come on."*

Then from outside came the sound of voices and thumping feet. The screen door banged open and my dad was beside me.

"What's happened, Cyril?" He grabbed Aunt Gertrude's wrist while I told him. Maggie came panting up the steps as my dad said, "Heat stroke, I bet. Cyril, get me the ice-cubes and some plastic bags from the kitchen, fast, then we'll get some towels in cold water. I'll get her to the sofa. Maggie, run back to Hummakers' and get them to call an ambulance, then get over to Flynns'. We might need their car if we can't get an ambulance. Go!" He bent down and picked Aunt Gertrude up under the knees and arms.

Maggie took off down the steps as I raced for the kitchen. I could hear her yelling to Mrs. Hummaker just coming up the path. "Put the ice in two bags," my dad called to me, "and bring it in."

I hauled the ice tray out of the freezer. There wasn't much. I tossed the cubes into plastic bags from the drawer as fast as I could. When I got back to the living-room my dad had Great Aunt Gertrude lying on the couch and he was hauling off her sweater.

"Good. That's a start." My dad grabbed the bags and put one under her arm and one on her forehead. "Now let's get those towels."

As we ran out through the kitchen to the clothes-line my dad slammed on the cold water. He ripped the towels down off the line into my arms and we stuffed them into the sink.

As fast as they got wet I ran them, cold and dripping in to my dad at the couch and he'd shift the ice around and put the towels on Aunt Gertrude.

"We have to get her temperature down," he said. "Here, lift her leg while I put this under – that's right – pass me that other towel. How long do you think she was like this before you found her?"

"Just a few minutes," I almost wailed. "Is it too late? Will it be – bad?"

"Hard to say," said my dad. "You can get brain damage from heat stroke. Even – well, it can be bad." He gave me a towel. "Here, soak this again."

There was a rap at the kitchen door and Mr. Flynn

swung in. "Car's out back if you need it."

My dad took the cold towel and passed me another warm one. "Thanks, Mike," he said. "We'd better wait until we find out about the ambulance. I just wish it wasn't so hot in here."

"Our place is the same," said Mr. Flynn. "You want to put her down in the lake?"

"It's probably best not to move her," my dad said, "but we could use some more ice. Have you got any?"

"A bag full," said Mr. Flynn. "Be right back."

Maggie passed him in the doorway. "Ambulance is coming," she called and then helped with towels. In a minute Mr. Flynn was back with ice and after that there was nothing to do but change towels and wait. I couldn't stand to be in there any more. I went outside where I could be by myself.

After a little while I heard the ambulance pull up and saw Maggie run by leading the men with the stretcher. Then everyone came out carrying Great Aunt Gertrude. She looked like an old, old lady going to die.

I stayed in the trees until Maggie found me. My dad had gone in the ambulance with Great Aunt Gertrude and my mom had come back from shopping and driven off after the ambulance, too. We were supposed to stay at Mr. Flynn's till they got back.

"Did you see her?" I whispered. "She looked..."

"She'll be okay, Cyril." Maggie didn't sound like she believed it, but there was nothing else to say.

Any other time hanging around at a cottage with Mr. Flynn and Joyce would have been too excellent to believe, but I didn't care a hill of beans. They bustled around saying it would be fine and heat stroke had happened to someone they knew and let's have lunch and go out in the canoe. But every time I'd start to forget and feel okay, *whump,* it would hit me again. I'd see Great Aunt Gertrude's face all red and saggy, and a sour, chokey feeling would fill up my insides and I'd feel *my* face twisting. Even when Maggie and Joyce trapped Mr. Flynn with the glass-on-the-ceiling trick I hardly even noticed.

I just kept thinking, what if her brain got hurt? Would she die? Nobody I knew ever died before. Great Aunt Gertrude got me pretty twitchy sometimes, but no way did I want her dead. And what if she died because it was me that could have saved her except I was too dumb to know what to do? Would I be like a murderer? I couldn't get the thought out of my mind. Canoeing didn't help, neither did landing and exploring up the beach.

By the time we hauled up the canoe back at the cottage they were all busy and cheery enough to be elves for Santa Claus. It was really nice of them, but I just couldn't feel better.

"Let's go for a swim," said Mr. Flynn. "C'mon, you two, we'll get my mask and snorkel and do it right."

We went up to the car and Mr. Flynn hunted around in the trunk. Maggie peered in beside him. I leaned against a tree and looked at where our car would come in. When would my parents get back with news? I wished it was soon, unless that meant – I shook my head and made myself listen to Maggie. "Hey," she was saying, "is that *two* tents in there?"

"Yup," said Mr. Flynn. "That's our old one. It might come in handy for storing things."

"I thought you said it leaked," Maggie said suspiciously.

"Well, the fly doesn't fit properly," Mr. Flynn said.

I walked away out past the trees and into the lane. Camping didn't seem so fun to me any more. Not if you could get hurt just being hot.

"Cyril," Maggie was calling. "Cyrillll." Then I heard another noise, just a tiny hum but getting louder and louder. "Wait," I yelled. "They're coming!" and then my mom and dad drove up the lane.

My heart began to thump. Then my dad was opening the door and saying, "She's all right, Cyril." I sort of jumped and he scooped me up and I didn't even mind. He bounced me back down and my mom squeezed me and I didn't mind that either. Then she gave me an extra hug and said it was from Aunt Gertrude. "She says she was lucky you were there. I already knew that," my mom said, and squeezed me again. That time I squirmed.

Then Maggie and Joyce and Mr. Flynn were there and my mom and dad were telling about everything. The doctor said Great Aunt Gertrude had heat stroke all right, but she'd be okay. She had to stay overnight in the hospital though, to make sure.

"She's one tough old bird," my dad said, smiling.

"She's lucky," Joyce said.

"Lucky you knew what to do, Arch," Mr. Flynn put in.

My dad grinned and waved his hand. "I did a file piece on heat stroke for the paper last summer. Where Cyril got his stuff is another question. That's where she was really lucky. If these two," he nodded at Maggie and me, "hadn't kept their heads and done exactly the right thing, she would have been in really big trouble."

I bit my cheeks in to keep from grinning too hard, then looked sideways at Maggie. She was trying to look as if she heard that kind of stuff all the time. Being Maple Avenue Marvel, maybe she did.

"Listen," Joyce said, "have you eaten? You guys must be starved."

"I bet you could use a beer," Mr. Flynn said.

"Could we," sighed my mom. "But you know what I really want? A swim." And in about three seconds flat it was all fixed up. Everyone was going to have a swim and something to drink over at our place, and then we'd have a barbecue.

So we finally got to go swimming. Well, Maggie and I and Joyce and my mom did. My dad and Mr. Flynn, they just swished the water with their arms and floated and sipped their beers and talked. Weird how grownups didn't like to splash around. Even weirder was what they talked about – books and writing and stuff. Not one word about camping or scuba diving or adventures or anything. There was

Mr. Flynn saying he was always trying to write and never got anywhere with it and asking my dad all these questions about books and papers and where to get stories published. And there was my dad flopped out on the air mattress like he owned the place, explaining things like they were easy as pie. And the weirdest part of all was, I *liked* it. Especially when my dad said how I helped him write his book. He even had a tan now that his sunburn had peeled.

When everybody finished swimming, Maggie and I stayed down on the beach while the grownups went up to get changed. After the cool water it felt nice to toast again in the heat from the sand. We skipped stones and Maggie beat me. It took her till best fifteen out of seventeen, though, because I was getting better at it after all that walking on the beach by myself. Then we flopped down on our towels.

"You'd better give Joyce some of those rocks, Cyril," Maggie reminded me.

"I will, I will," I said, not really listening.

"Don't forget," Maggie said, "because our plan's going to work even better now."

I should have asked why, but I was more interested in the voices and laughter coming from the lawn. I felt like hanging around with the adults and talking grownup. "Let's go up and change," I said.

We raced to the cottage. I won. Maggie said it didn't count because I didn't call "Race you!" until I was way ahead of her going to the stairs. I was first changed though, fair and square. Maggie wasted too much time talking about stuff she was going to do tomorrow. I just kept saying "Uh-huh," skipped my socks and went out into the living-room still pulling on my T-shirt.

"Wait up," Maggie called from her room, so I bounced on the scratchy couch and listened to the voices from outside.

At first they were talking about Great Aunt Gertrude, but then out of nowhere, I heard Mr. Flynn say, "By the way, you know what else happened today? I found out that Cyril was behind the class getting us that tent. Maggie told me." I bounced off the couch so fast I almost broke my neck.

"Geez, that was the biggest thing since sliced bread around our place for a while," my dad chuckled. "Mr. Flynn this and Mr. Flynn that and I hope he likes the colour and I wish it was bigger." I felt my face beginning to burn. "And then," my dad went on, like it was one hilarious joke, "when he didn't take it and I had to go running all over town to Jan's school, then yours – "

"You mean you had the present? Then that whole riddle thing was a stall!" Mr. Flynn hooted. "But wait a minute. Cyril had that box before you got there!"

"Riddle?" asked my mom.

"No," my dad interrupted, "he had the *other* box. He gave that one to me and I gave him the tent."

"Other box?" asked Mr. Flynn, and then it all came out, the bikini and everything. I thought they were going to break their chairs laughing. I wanted to bury myself inside the couch. Just when I was feeling grown up. I'd thought I wanted Mr. Flynn to know I got him the tent but now it sounded so dumb, little kid stuff. And after I'd been snuffling around all day like a sucky baby, too. Mr. Flynn would figure that Maggie told him so he'd pat me on the head. Even worse, he'd figure I wanted him to. I groaned out loud and found Maggie standing beside me.

"You blabbed!" I hissed. "Now he's going to think I'm a crybaby. Thanks a whole bunch!"

"No he won't, Cyril," Maggie whispered back. "Don't you get it? I had to, to help – " Her voice disappeared in whoops of laughter from outside.

"A *duel*?" My mom was laughing so hard she could barely talk. "I remember him covered with rotten egg, but that's not what he told ... told .... " She gasped and laughed all over again.

"Shhhhhh," my dad said. "They'll hear."

"Well, that's what he told me," Joyce said in a low voice. "When we were collecting stones on the beach."

"You'd be surprised what's news to us," my dad said.

Joyce said, "Well, apparently Maggie and Russell outsmarted each other with this trick about hard-boiled eggs." Then she told my parents the whole story I'd told her. I almost turned into a toad. They laughed their heads off and Maggie was glaring at me.

"You," she breathed, "told." She made "told" sound like the most evil word in the universe. "Cyril, you disgusting betrayer!" She was so mad I forgot I was mad at her.

"I didn't mean it," I pleaded, and said the only thing I could think of. "I had to. Like you."

Maggie burned at me with her lips jammed together and her eyes all squinched up. "You mean you had the same idea?"

"Yeah," I said, really fast. Then I hoped really hard. It worked. Maggie plopped down beside me on the couch and sighed.

"Well, I guess it didn't do much good, did it?" she said. I couldn't tell, seeing as how I still didn't know what the idea was. I didn't say anything.

Maggie said, "I'm not going out there now. I'd feel like an idiot."

"Me either," I said.

Outside they were still talking. Mr. Flynn said, "No, really, I'll be back in a minute." We heard his footsteps go by the window.

"What do you want to do?" I asked.

"I don't feel like doing anything. What about you?"

"Nah," I said. So we sat there. Joyce and my mom were talking about where they'd been camping, but I didn't listen very hard. I just hoped no one came inside.

In a couple of minutes we heard whistling and footsteps coming by the window again. Then there was whispering and they all called for us to come outside.

We looked at each other. "We better go," Maggie said, so we hauled ourselves up and shuffled outside as if it were time for a math test. They were all sitting in lawn chairs, except for Mr. Flynn. He was standing up, holding a blue bag with a drawstring. He was wearing his floppy straw hat again and his moustache curled up even higher than ever.

"Well, hey," he said, "there you are. Cyril, I just found out that it was you who got everybody to buy Joyce and me that great new tent, and I've never thanked you for it. I should have known you'd be too modest to mention it."

I blinked. Modest? Didn't he think I was a sucky baby, that the whole thing was silly? I almost blabbed, "We heard you laughing," but something stopped me. If Mr. Flynn wasn't going to say he laughed, I wasn't going to say I'd heard.

"And Maggie," Mr. Flynn went on, "I've heard that you two are looking for a new clubhouse. Now I know that you've probably got something all planned, but Joyce and I thought we'd offer you our old tent anyway, to use if you want it."

"Absolutely," said Joyce. "That nice new one is plenty for us."

"Let it be our way of thanking you for, well, ... for ... keeping things hopping," Mr. Flynn finished up.

Maggie said it for both of us: "All riggght!"

And it was.

After the barbecue that night I spread my whole rock collection out on the floor of the tent. We'd set

116

it up right away, of course, after the thank-yous. While we'd worked, Maggie whispered that our plan had worked after all. At first I didn't get it, but then I knew what she meant. Maggie hadn't told Mr. Flynn about the gift just to get him to thank me and make me feel better. When she'd spotted the second tent, she'd started hoping we might get it if she hinted right. And she was sure I'd had the same reason for telling about the egg-tossing duel and how the garbage truck got the Vulkoviches' boxes.

"You know what Aunt Gertrude said, Cyril," she whispered, and whacked extra hard at a tent peg, "great minds think the same. So you know what? We can keep the tent at your place as long as we put it up in my yard every other week."

"Really?"

"Really. Partners?"

"For sure." I took the hammer for the next peg. It all sounded so good I decided not to tell Maggie she got Aunt Gertrude's saying wrong.

"But," Maggie said, "you've got to tell me one thing: How did you know they had both tents in the car way back then?"

"Huh?" I hammered the ground instead of the tent peg. "I, well, I …. " I didn't know. Then I remembered my new Cyril rule for being a genius. I shut my mouth and smiled.

"Oh Cyril, you sneak!" Maggie complained, but she was grinning. "Okay, I'll figure it out for myself."

I smiled again, a sort of go-ahead-and-try kind of

smile, and went back to hammering. I really was smarter with my mouth shut.

And I'd kept it shut too, when it was important, all the way through dinner, right up till now when nobody would hear me. The way the setting sun was shining through the blue walls of the tent the rocks looked almost as if they were under water again. Outside, down at the real water I could hear the others taking a last quick swim. I reached back and pulled the front flap of the tent closed. I wanted to be alone while I did this one last plan. It wasn't super brilliant or anything, but I wanted it all to myself.

I pulled four socks out of my pockets and laid them out on the crinkly plastic floor. Humming the cottage song, I picked the rocks that would go in each, one by one, a pile for Joyce and Mr. Flynn, some for my dad, some for my mom and some extra good ones for Great Aunt Gertrude. When I was done there was a sock full of rocks for each of them. Then I pulled out one last sock and put the piece of beach glass in it. That was for Maggie. I heaped all the socks together on one side of the tent. The rest of the rocks fit in my backpack with room left over.

When I was done, I stretched out in the warm blue light of our tent. A cricket was already chirping. The friendly voices were still murmuring from the water and birds were calling. When everybody came up I was going to ask them the difference between unlawful and illegal, but right now I was taking a rest. After all, there was still a lot of summer left.